Kate Saunders worked as a  twenty-five and then becar
author of six novels for adults and has edited one
collection of short stories. The very successful
Belfry Witches series had a major BBC TV series
based on it, and she is also the author of *Cat and
the Stinkwater War*, described by *The Times* as
'lively and delightful'.

As a journalist she has worked for the *Sunday
Times*, the *Daily Telegraph*, the *Independent* and
the *Sunday Express*. She can also be heard
regularly on BBC Radio 4. She lives with her
family (and three cats) in London.

Also by Kate Saunders

Cat and the Stinkwater War

The Belfry Witches

Fly Again

Kate Saunders
Illustrated by Tony Ross

MACMILLAN CHILDREN'S BOOKS

Power Hat Panic, Witch You Were Here and *Broomsticks in Space* first published 2000 by Macmillan Children's Books

This edition published 2005 by Macmillan Children's Books
a division of Macmillan Publishers Limited
20 New Wharf Road, London N1 9RR
Basingstoke and Oxford
www.panmacmillan.co.uk

Associated companies throughout the world

ISBN 0 330 43610 4

1 3 5 7 9 8 6 4 2

A CIP catalogue record for this book is available from the British Library.

Typeset by SX Composing DTP, Rayleigh, Essex
Printed and bound in Great Britain by Mackays of Chatham plc, Kent

Contents

Power Hat Panic

For my nephews Tom and George

1

The Old Bag is Dead

It was a bright autumn morning in the quiet village of Tranters End, but Skirty Marm could not enjoy it. She was in one of her Moods.

"It's NOT FAIR!" she thundered. "What's the point of choosing two witches to be godmothers, if you won't let them give the baby a magic present?"

Old Noshie was sitting on her cushion, comfortably eating a bowl of flaked bats for her breakfast. "We promised Mr B.," she reminded her friend. "No more magic without written permission, unless it's an emergency."

"POOH!" shouted Skirty Marm. She began to pace up and down across the dusty floor of the church belfry where the two witches lived. "Everyone else will give Thomas boring rattles and shawls. I wanted to give that baby something really special!"

The baby in question was Thomas William Babbercorn. He belonged to Mr Cuthbert Babbercorn, the young curate at St Tranter's Church, and his wife, Alice. Ever since Old Noshie and Skirty Marm had been thrown off Witch Island, Mr Babbercorn had been their best human friend. They loved Alice very nearly as much – they had been her bridesmaids, and a copy of the wedding photograph was taped to one of the huge church bells that hung above the witches' heads. Until the thrilling arrival of Thomas, it had been the happiest day of the witches' lives.

"I thought of another perfect gift last night," Skirty Marm said. "What if we gave Thomas the power to make himself INVISIBLE?"

Old Noshie was impressed. She always admired Skirty's ideas (sometimes with unfortunate consequences).

"Thomas would like that," she said slowly, thinking it over. "Especially when he gets bigger. If he didn't want to go to school one morning, he could just vanish!" She sighed, then shook her head. "But I don't think Alice would like having a vanishing baby. I think we should give Thomas the power to make himself FLY."

2

"You old fool!" snapped Skirty Marm. "She certainly doesn't want a flying baby. What if he fell asleep while he was on the ceiling? Alice and Mr B. would keep having to fetch the ladder!"

"Drat, I didn't think of that," Old Noshie said humbly.

"That's just your trouble," Skirty Marm said, in a stern voice. "You don't THINK, Noshie."

"I never was much good at it," admitted Old Noshie.

She was a plump easy-going witch, with startling, bright green skin. Her wrinkled head was completely bald, and she wore a blue wig under her pointed hat, to keep it warm. At Witch School she had trundled along at the bottom of the class, quite content to be in the shadow of her brilliant friend and cave-mate, Skirty Marm.

Skirty Marm was long and skinny. Her skin was grey, her eyes were red, and her hair was purple. When she was angry, or thinking very hard, sparks shot out of the ends of her hair. At school, she had won all kinds of dazzling prizes, including the Spellbinder's Medal for thirty-six years in a row. She never could accept Mr Babbercorn's strict "No Magic" rule.

"Cheer up, Skirt!" urged Old Noshie. "We'll be able to buy Thomas something lovely with all the human money we've saved. Our money-box is filling up nicely." She rattled the box, which was shaped like a little thatched cottage.

Mr Babbercorn had given them permission to use very mild magic, so that they could earn some human money by doing odd jobs for the people of the village. Mostly, this meant flying up to roofs on their broomsticks, and clearing blocked gutters or fixing television aerials. It was all rather a come-down for an award-winning Spellbinder like Skirty Marm.

She opened her mouth to insult Old Noshie. At that moment, however, something black and smoky suddenly crashed through the open belfry window.

Both witches coughed and spluttered as a cloud of smoke covered everything in a fine layer of black soot. When the smoke cleared, they saw a battered newspaper lying in the middle of the floor.

"Well I never!" cried Skirty Marm, forgetting to be cross. "It's the *Witch Island Courier*!"

This was the national newspaper of Witch

4

Island, the bleak and rocky land where the two witches had once lived.

Old Noshie squeaked and hid behind her friend – she was rather a coward. "What does it mean, Skirt? Who sent it?"

Skirty Marm was very brave. "It's been sent by Super-Express, and you know how much that costs," she said. "This must be something important."

She picked up the newspaper – still warm from its magical expressing – and opened it out.

"Aaargh!" yelled Old Noshie, her blue wig bristling with shock.

Plastered across the front page was a photograph of a disgusting old witch, with metal teeth and a coarse grey beard.

"Mrs Abercrombie," Skirty Marm said bitterly. "Our worst enemy!" Then her grey skin turned a dirty white. "Noshie! Look at the headline! 'EX-QUEEN VANISHES IN TUNNEL DISASTER!'"

In a shaking voice, she read out the story.

"The Witch Island Police yesterday gave up the search for disgraced former queen Mrs Abercrombie, reported missing after the shock collapse of three disused underground tunnels.

'It's now pretty certain that Mrs A. was trapped in one of the tunnels,' said our respected leader, Chancellor Badsleeves. 'And all sensible witches will rejoice that the nasty old bag is dead.'

Mrs Abercrombie, who wasted all her money trying to win back power, had been teaching at Witch-School to make ends meet. The alarm was raised when she failed to turn up for her favourite lesson, Punishment Hour. She was known to keep an underground vault near the site of the disaster.

Chancellor Badsleeves described her dis-

appearance as 'the end of an era', and added that there would be a State Funeral, with fireworks and dancing afterwards."

There was a long long silence. This was an incredible piece of news. The wicked former queen of Witch Island, who had sworn to kill Old Noshie and Skirty Marm, was dead. The two witches were only jolted out of their gaping astonishment when the church bells struck eleven, making the whole tower shake. As soon as the racket died away, Skirty Marm cried "HURRAH!" and turned sixteen cartwheels.

Old Noshie, too fat for cartwheels, did eleven somersaults and stood on her head (I should explain that though they were over one hundred and fifty years old, this is an extremely young and sprightly age for a witch). Then she got out some mouldy sausage rolls she had been saving for a special celebration. Celebrations did not come more special than this one.

The late Mrs Abercrombie had hated Old Noshie and Skirty Marm. She had banished them from Witch Island for singing a rude song about her at the Hallowe'en Ball. That was bad enough. They had led the Revolution that ended her cruel reign, and that was terrible. But it was not the worst thing they had done to her.

They had stolen the Power Hat.

The Power Hat was a pointed hat, two metres tall, with an everlasting candle burning at its tip. A gale could blow and a flood of water pour down on it, but this candle never went out. The Hat was immensely magic, and anyone who wore it had incredible power. Skirty and Noshie had snatched the Power Hat from the unsavoury head of Mrs Abercrombie and hidden it in Tranters End. The ex-queen had tried to win it back, but had always failed.

These days, it was disguised as a black-and-white bobble hat, which made it far easier to hide. It lived quietly in Mr Babbercorn's underwear drawer, bothering nobody. Since its arrival among the humans it was a changed Hat. It had, to Mrs Abercrombie's disgust, turned Good.

"Badsleeves must have sent that paper," said Skirty Marm. The democratically elected Chancellor of Witch Island was an old friend of the two witches. "Good old Baddy! We must go back to Witch Island for the funeral – I bet that'll be the best party ever!"

Old Noshie was thoughtful. "We could go

back to LIVE there if we wanted," she mused. "Her magic can't reach us now she's been squashed like a big fat beetle."

Skirty Marm scornfully tossed her purple hair. "I don't mind visiting the Island, but I wouldn't live there again – not if they gave us a luxury cave, with hot and cold running slime. It's much nicer here."

"I'd be homesick for the humans," Old Noshie agreed. "We were so frightened of being banished, but it was actually the best thing that ever happened to us."

The witches had grown to love living in an English village. Because of their strange mixture of ages – very old for humans, very young for witches – they had joined both the Brownies and the Old Folks' Drop-In Club. They could not make up their minds which they liked best. Skirty Marm loved to look at the Old Folks' photograph albums, and hear their stories about human history. Old Noshie's Brownie badge for tying knots was the first prize she had ever won – she was so proud of it, she had sewn it to her vest.

"I miss my spellbook, though," Skirty Marm said. "And my red stockings. The new ones

Brown Owl made for us just aren't the same."

I should explain that on Witch Island, a witch's stockings are her pride and joy. You can tell the age and status of a witch by the colour of her stockings. A baby witch, under one hundred years old, wears yellow stockings and learns Elementary Magic at Witch School. At the age of one hundred, a witch becomes a Red-Stocking. She is given a broom, a share of a cave and the Red-Stocking spellbook. On her two hundredth birthday the stockings become green, and the spellbook is more advanced. Finally, at the age of three hundred, a witch becomes a Purple-Stocking and is licensed to cast the most powerful spells of all.

Mrs Abercrombie had been the oldest, cleverest and wickedest Purple on the Island. During the seven centuries of her reign, the Purples had kept talking cats as slaves and bullied the younger witches – especially the Red-Stockings, who had a reputation for being cheeky and disobedient. Nowadays, the country was led by the Red-Stocking Badsleeves, the cat-slaves were free, and the Greens and Purples had to behave. They would probably behave even better now that their old leader had been squashed by a collapsing tunnel.

"I've missed this cookery page," Old Noshie said, leafing through the *Witch Island Courier*. "Look – a delicious recipe for Ant Crumble. You soften the ants in diesel-oil, add a grated conker—"

"Stop thinking of your stomach," said Skirty Marm, snatching the paper. "Let's go and tell Mr B. the good news!"

Mr Babbercorn and his vicar, Mr Snelling, had met the late Mrs Abercrombie. It had not been a pleasant experience.

"Great idea," Old Noshie said. "Won't he be pleased to hear that he never needs to worry about Mrs A. ever again?"

The two joyous witches ran down the one hundred and eighty-six belfry steps to the vicarage next door. In the kitchen, they found the curate and his wife. Mr Babbercorn, a pale and somewhat weedy young man, was making a cup of tea. His wife Alice, a sweet-faced young woman with curly brown hair, was putting baby clothes into the washing machine. Baby Thomas was asleep in his carrycot.

"Morning, witches," said Alice.

"Have some tea," said Mr Babbercorn. He

11

poured them each a cup of warm water and added a spoonful of soil from the potted geranium on the windowsill – he knew the witches could not abide human tea.

Old Noshie and Skirty Marm were far too excited to drink anything. Both talking at the same time, they blurted out the amazing news.

Mr Babbercorn was so shocked, he had to sit down. "That terrible evil witch – dead!"

"I know it's wrong to feel happy," Alice said, "but it's such a relief!"

Mrs Abercrombie had once turned Alice into a snail, and Alice still had ghastly dreams about finding herself with a pair of tiny horns and a shell again.

There was a squawk from the carrycot.

"Hello, Thomas," said Old Noshie.

"He wants to talk to us," said Skirty Marm.

Mr Babbercorn and Alice smiled at each other. The witches claimed that there was a language called "Babyspeak", which enabled them to talk to Thomas. His parents (though they should have known better) found this very difficult to believe. Mothers and fathers – even when they have friends who are witches – think nobody understands their baby better than they do. And the noises the witches made at Thomas sounded ridiculous.

"It's a shame you don't know Babyspeak," said Old Noshie. "Would you like us to give you a few lessons?"

Alice picked up her baby. "No thanks."

Over her shoulder, the red and crumpled face of Thomas looked as if it was trying to smile at the witches.

He made a noise, which sounded like "ARRR!"

Skirty Marm replied: "Aaar-EE!"

If Alice and Mr Babbercorn had understood Babyspeak, they would have known that Thomas was saying: "Hello, witches – isn't it a lovely morning?"

And they would have heard Skirty Marm saying: "Hello, Thomas. I hope we didn't wake you."

"Not at all," said Thomas. "I just can't settle today – I've got wind."

"Poor thing," said Alice, "he can't settle today. He's got wind."

(Perhaps she did not need to learn Babyspeak after all.)

She put Thomas into his little bouncy chair.

"Drat, she's putting me in that chair!" complained Thomas.

"She's got to finish her tea," Old Noshie pointed out, in Babyspeak. "Do be reasonable. She can't hold you all the time."

"WHY NOT?" shouted Thomas.

Alice kissed his head, which was as bald as Old Noshie's.

"Come on, crosspatch! It's only for a minute."

"Oh, all right," said Thomas. "If you get me my plastic horses."

"Maybe he wants his horses," said Alice. She found his string of coloured horses and clipped them to the bouncy chair.

"She learns very quickly, bless her," Thomas told the witches.

Mr Babbercorn was thinking about Mrs Abercrombie. "It wouldn't be suitable to celebrate," he murmured. "After all, it is a tragedy. Maybe I should hold a service of thanksgiving?"

The back door opened and in walked Mendax.

"This shopping weighs a ton. I need a nice sit-down and a saucer of milk."

14

Mendax was a small black cat. He had once been a cat-slave on Witch Island, and Mrs Abercrombie had sent him to Tranters End as a spy. Old Noshie and Skirty Marm had now forgiven him for his shady past (though Skirty was still a little suspicious), and Mr Snelling had adopted him. Mendax was very bossy and ruled the soft-hearted vicar with a paw of iron, but the two were devoted to each other.

Mendax was an extremely useful cat. He cooked brilliantly, polished the furniture, and did light shopping. Mr Snelling had given him a little blue cart, which he could drag along the village street. Everyone in Tranters End was now quite used to meeting Mendax in Mrs Tucker's Post Office and General Shop. He was a great gossip and knew everything that went on in the village.

"The old woodman's cottage in the forest has been sold," he mewed, lifting a packet of nappies out of his cart. "Nobody has seen the lady who bought it, but Mrs Tucker says she's very rich and rather delicate."

Thomas squawked again. This meant: "I bet that's one of your LIES!"

In Latin, Mendax means "Liar" – and the name suited the little cat perfectly. He was absolutely addicted to telling tall stories. When people pointed this out, however, he was always offended.

"My dear Thomas," he purred in Babyspeak, "when you know me better, you will realize I am the SOUL of TRUTH."

"Never mind that broken-down old cottage!" cried Skirty Marm. "We've got a REAL piece of news." And she slammed down the *Witch Island Courier*.

When Mendax saw the headline, his fur stood on end. He began to tremble all over.

16

"Dead? Mrs Abercrombie? Oh, it's too wonderful! I hardly dare to believe it!"

"We should have a party," said Old Noshie. "With nice games and funny hats."

Mr Babbercorn was uneasy. "I really don't think that would be in the best of taste—" he began.

"Pooh to the best of taste!" said Mendax, recovering. He took his apron off its low hook beside the door. "I'll start the cake now! What do you fancy, witches – strawberry or chocolate?"

17

2

Mrs Brightpie

Mr Babbercorn felt rather guilty about being so happy, but nobody else did. Even the vicar, podgy Mr Snelling, who was one of the kindest men in the world, treated the fatal squashing of Mrs Abercrombie as a fine excuse for a party.

"I'm afraid I can't help it," he told Mr Babbercorn firmly. "Vicars aren't supposed to be pleased about things like this – but ever since that horrid old witch smashed her way into my house, I've been terrified that she'll come back. Now that she's gone, I'm just thankful to be safe."

"I never liked the idea that she might be using her spells to spy on us," admitted Mr Babbercorn. "The fact is, if people want anyone to be sorry at their funerals, they should be nicer when they're alive."

"Very true," said Mr Snelling. "I may get

Mendax to write me a sermon about it."

The sermons the vicar wrote himself were dull and waffly. The people of Tranters End had been delighted when Mendax started writing them instead. Mendax's sermons were sometimes rather far-fetched, but they were never boring.

"In the meantime," Mr Snelling went on, "let the witches have their celebration. Tell them they can play loud music on their transistor radio, and put fairy-lights on the bells."

Mendax cooked a splendid feast of cake, trifle and caramelized cockroaches, and danced with the witches far into the night.

This was the beginning of a very happy time at Tranters End. The October weather was as mild as spring. The autumn woods were every shade of red. Mr Babbercorn found himself singing as he delivered parish magazines. Mendax told fewer lies, the witches only quarrelled twice a day and Mr Snelling decided to hold a grand Harvest Supper.

"We need to raise some money for a new organ," he said, "and people always enjoy a feast. I'm hoping Mrs Brightpie will come."

Mrs Brightpie was the lady who had bought the ruined cottage in the middle of the woods.

She was a pretty old lady, with snow-white hair, pink cheeks and blue eyes. Though she looked delicate and walked with the help of a stick, she was very energetic and cheerful.

The cottage was right at the heart of the thick forest, but for several weeks lorries had been bringing in bricks and cement, and huge diggers had been squeezing down the narrow woodland paths. Mrs Brightpie was rich and she was turning the tumbledown old place into a dream home stuffed with luxuries.

Not that anyone in the village had seen it yet.

"I don't want to show it off until it's completely finished," Mrs Brightpie had laughed, while she was buying stamps from Mrs Tucker at the post office. "Then I'll hold a big housewarming party!"

Everyone looked forward to this. Mrs Brightpie had only been in Tranters End for a short time, but her kindness and generosity had made her very popular. She had bought a new papier-mâché toadstool for the Brownies to dance round, after the top fell off the old one. She had given the church a beautiful new tea urn, and she kept the Old Folks' Drop-In Club supplied with delicious biscuits (greedy old

Noshie, who loved human biscuits, was particularly pleased about this).

"What a super idea!" Mrs Brightpie exclaimed, when Mr Snelling told her about the Harvest Supper. "Of course I'll come – and I'll start off that organ fund with two hundred pounds!"

She would not let the vicar thank her.

"Nonsense, Mr Snelling. I have plenty to spare, and I believe in sharing. I want to do some good in this charming village."

Mrs Tucker said Mrs Brightpie was "a ray of sunshine".

Mr Snelling said, "How lucky we are, to have a kind-hearted neighbour like Mrs Brightpie!"

Mr Babbercorn and Alice liked her because she kissed Thomas and gave him a little velvet dinosaur.

Old Noshie and Skirty Marm liked her because she had not been at all shocked when the vicar explained about the two local witches and the talking cat.

"How fascinating!" she had cried, in her silvery voice. "I certainly don't mind a touch of magic. I shall enjoy chatting with Mendax. And Old Noshie and Skirty Marm must have tea with me, to tell me all about being witches!"

Since Mrs Brightpie's house was not ready yet, she held her special witches' tea at the vicarage. They were a little shy at first – Old Noshie, in particular, found human table manners very hard work, and they both wanted to make a good impression on the refined Mrs Brightpie.

But it was impossible to be shy for long. Mrs Brightpie was so interested and so sympathetic that they were soon treating her like an old friend. They even sang her "A Nasty Old Thing" – the rude song about Mrs Abercrombie that had got them banished from Witch Island.

"Goodness, how amusing!" laughed Mrs Brightpie. "I bet she was cross!"

"That's nothing!" boasted Old Noshie. "We stole her Power Hat!"

Mrs Brightpie handed her another chocolate biscuit. "Gosh, you must be very clever witches! What did you do with it?"

"We hid it in—" began Old Noshie.

Skirty Marm nudged her. "We'd better not tell you," she said quickly. "The Hat's a dangerous thing to know about."

Mrs Brightpie smiled. "Surely it doesn't matter, now that your queen is dead?"

"Some other witch might be after it," Skirty Marm said darkly. "And we'd hate to get you into trouble."

"You're very considerate," said Mrs Brightpie. For a moment she looked thoughtful. Then she smiled again and started talking about the Brownies. This was Old Noshie's favourite subject and she quickly forgot about the Power Hat.

"We always have a LOVELY time at Brownies," she told Mrs Brightpie. "And guess what – I've got a badge for tying knots. Look!"

She pulled out her vest, so that Mrs Brightpie could see it.

Skirty Marm nudged her again. "Stop flashing your vest! Don't you know it's RUDE to show your underwear at table?" She turned back to Mrs Brightpie. "The other Brownies sew their badges to their uniforms – but they're tiny little human girlies. You can't get Brownie uniforms in witch-sizes."

"What a shame!" cried Mrs Brightpie. "I shall have some specially made for you!"

The witches were thunderstruck. Old Noshie was so thrilled, her mouth dropped open and bits of half-chewed cake fell on the tea-table.

"REAL Brownie uniforms?" she gasped. This was a dream come true. Every time she went to Brownies, Old Noshie longed for a smart yellow shirt and thought how elegant her bald green head would look in the brown hat.

"Of course!" said Mrs Brightpie. "No – don't try to thank me! I'm looking for nice things to do in this village."

After this, Old Noshie and Skirty Marm absolutely loved Mrs Brightpie and thought her one of the very kindest humans they had ever met. And she kept her promise. Two specially made Brownie uniforms arrived at the vicarage three days later, and when Old Noshie put on her brown trousers and yellow shirt, there was no prouder Brownie in the world.

"Such a generous lady!" Mendax said approvingly to the witches. "And so broad-minded." He liked Mrs Brightpie, mainly because she was a new audience for his tall stories. "She was very sympathetic about my terrible war-wound from the Battle of Fungus Gulch. When I described how I begged the doctor to help the others first, she almost wept!"

Skirty Marm rolled her eyes wearily. "For the last time – you weren't at Fungus Gulch. It happened before you were born."

Mendax tossed his head. "Mrs Brightpie says I have a natural talent for storytelling, and she's promised to help me write my memoirs. She says everyone should be encouraged to use their talents."

This piece of wisdom made Skirty Marm very thoughtful. That evening, when the two witches were sitting on their cushions in the belfry, listening to their transistor radio by candlelight, she announced, "Noshie, I've been thinking.

Mrs Brightpie was right. People should be allowed to use their talents."

"Yes," Old Noshie agreed, "I've got a talent for making fizzy drinks come down my nose – but Alice won't let me use it. She says it's RUDE."

Skirty Marm ignored this. "Our talent is for making magic – let's face it, we're not much good at anything else. I think we should use it to give Thomas a proper christening present."

"It's no use," said Old Noshie. "Mr B. says his mind is made up. He'll never let us cast spells on his baby."

"Pooh!" cried Skirty Marm. "Why do we have to tell him? He won't even find out until Thomas learns to talk Hinglish. And then he'll be GRATEFUL."

Old Noshie gasped. This was a very daring and shocking idea. It was one of the naughtiest things Skirty Marm had ever suggested – and she couldn't help liking it.

"If Mr B. was a king in a fairy story," Skirty Marm went on, "instead of a curate, he'd be very glad to have a few good spells at his baby's christening. So we'd really be doing him a favour!"

"Well . . ." Old Noshie said. She loved the idea, but needed to be talked into it. She was not a brave witch and disobeying Mr Babbercorn was a serious matter.

Skirty Marm leapt off her cushion and began to pace up and down across the moonlit floorboards. This was a sure sign that her genius was working furiously.

"It would have to be a very safe present," she said, "and something that didn't show. Put the kettle on, Nosh – let's make a list."

Old Noshie made cups of warm gutter-water, and the two witches settled down with crayons and paper. They discussed and argued and biffed each other all night, until pale dawn crept into the belfry. Finally, they had a list of four possible secret magic gifts to give Thomas:

1. The Gift of never being stuck in a traffic jam.
2. The Gift of making perfect excuses.
3. The Gift of understanding animals.
4. The Gift of twisting long balloons into sausage-dogs.

"Number Four is a load of RUBBISH!" Skirty Marm said scornfully.

Old Noshie stuck out her lip stubbornly. "I

saw a man do it on the vicar's telly. It was brilliant."

"You silly old bat!" Skirty Marm said. "What use will that be to Thomas? Nobody ever became Prime Minister because they could make sausage-dogs out of long balloons! I think we should give him Number One."

"We'd get found out!" shouted Old Noshie. "Alice would GUESS, the minute her car flew over a traffic jam!"

"All right," growled Skirty Marm. "We should go for Number Two – think how useful it'll be when Thomas starts school! He could say the dog ate his homework, and his teachers would believe him!" She sighed heavily. "Trouble is, making excuses is too much like LYING. Mr B. would be very cross with us, and I should hate that."

"Number Three is lovely," Old Noshie said. "Mr B. and Alice might even be pleased. Thomas would be able to talk to the animals, just like Doctor Don'tsmall."

"You mean DR DOLITTLE, you clot!" Skirty Marm biffed Old Noshie to organize her muddled thoughts. "Right then. We'll give Thomas Number Three. It's a tough spell –

but only the best is good enough for our godson!"

The spell was in two parts – a potion and a long poem. Skirty Marm's main job was remembering the poem. It was full of peculiar words in witch-Latin, the ancient language of spells. She and Old Noshie collected the ingredients for the potion. For several nights, they rode around the fields and hedges on their broomsticks, filling their hats with scraps of fur and feathers and bits of insects. They also caught the cries of various animals and stored them in the shell of a hazelnut.

They boiled the potion for three days and three nights until it had bubbled down to a tiny drop, smaller than the head of a pin. Then they took this round to the vicarage and looked for a chance to cast their spell without Mr Babbercorn or Alice seeing (they had both forgotten what a wicked thing they were doing – Skirty Marm said it was fine, because they "meant well").

Their chance came when Alice went to answer the telephone, leaving the witches alone in the vicarage kitchen with Thomas. Quick as a flash, Skirty Marm gabbled the poem, while Old

Noshie dabbed the potion on the bottom of Thomas's little fat foot.

"What are you doing?" Thomas cried, in Babyspeak.

"Don't worry," Old Noshie said. "It's a present for you."

Thomas was teething. He sat in his bouncy chair, chewing the velvet dinosaur from Mrs Brightpie. Suddenly, he threw it across the room and shouted, "I can hear TALKING! There's two beetles having a chat under the floorboards!"

The witches beamed – it had worked.

"I shouldn't think they're having a very interesting conversation," Skirty Marm said, "but you can switch it off if you get bored."

"Listen!" cried Thomas. "I can hear the words the birds are singing outside. This present is WONDERFUL!"

"Don't mention it," Old Noshie said modestly. "But we'd be grateful if you didn't tell your parents – well, you can't yet. But it's a secret."

Alice came back into the room and smiled to see her baby so radiantly happy.

"You two always cheer him up!" she said.

"I'm glad I chose you to be his godmothers."

Skirty Marm and Old Noshie giggled, and nudged each other hard – little did Alice know what brilliant godmothers they really were.

Next morning, Alice met Mrs Brightpie outside the post office.

"Hello, Mrs Brightpie," said Alice. "How are you?"

"Hello, Mrs Babbercorn," said Mrs Brightpie. "I'm extremely well, thank you." She bent over the buggy and smiled her sweet smile at Thomas. "And how is this lovely little boy of yours?"

Thomas was kicking and squawking under his blanket. The tabby cat from the post office sat beside him on the windowsill, staring into his face. When Thomas gave a loud squawk, the cat mewed.

"He's so fond of animals," Alice said fondly. "Anyone would think they were TALKING to each other!"

Mrs Brightpie was thoughtful. There was a moment of silence before she laughed and said she must be getting on.

3

A Disappearance

The peaceful time ended one week before the Harvest Supper. Mr Babbercorn was sitting quietly in the vicarage kitchen, drinking coffee and reading the *Church Times*, when he heard a terrible cry from the study.

He ran in at once – and found the vicar slumped against the desk, his round face almost grey with shock.

"What is it?" gasped Mr Babbercorn. "What on earth has happened?"

He had never seen the plump cheery vicar so upset.

Alice had also heard the terrible cry and came dashing downstairs. Together, she and her husband helped Mr Snelling into a chair.

"It must be my fault . . ." he murmured in a broken voice. "Something I said or did . . ."

There was a sheet of paper crumpled in his

fist. Mr Babbercorn took it and smoothed it out on the desk. He and Alice instantly recognized the neat spiky paw-writing of Mendax.

My Dear Mr Snelling,

By the time you read this, I shall be far away. I have been forced to leave Tranters End – I cannot say why, and it is better for everyone if NOBODY KNOWS WHERE I AM. Do not try to look for me.

It breaks my heart to leave you, dear vicar. Before I met you, I had no idea such kindness existed. You took a poor lying cat-slave and showed him the meaning of Goodness. I shall take this with me into my new life – wherever that may be. Think of me sometimes when you eat a jam tart. I shall always be thinking of you,

Your loving sorrowing cat,
MENDAX

PS I was going to give my little blue cart to the cat at the post office, but I fear he has not the intelligence to use it. Save it for Thomas – and give him a lick from his furry friend M.

PPS This letter does not contain a single LIE.

The letter was in typical flowery Mendax style, but it was splashed with watery blots that looked like tears. Mr Babbercorn and Alice stared at it in dismay.

What would the poor vicar do without his adored talking cat? Who would poach his eggs the way he liked, write his sermons and clean the chocolate-stains off his glasses?

And – the greatest question of all – why had Mendax done this?

"It's nothing to do with you," Alice assured Mr Snelling. "He says he was *forced* to leave – I think something terrible must have happened."

Mr Snelling blew his nose with a forlorn, honking sound that was very moving. "I'd better call PC Bloater – and perhaps if I put a notice in the newspapers and offer a reward—"

Mr Babbercorn shook his head. "Mendax says we mustn't try to look for him. And this isn't a job for the police – I'll fetch Old Noshie and Skirty Marm."

"Yes, this is serious," Skirty Marm said, when she had read the letter several times. "Mendax wouldn't leave this vicarage unless he really, truly had to—" She broke off to pinch Old

Noshie's nose. "Stop that grizzling!"

Old Noshie had not been much of a comfort to poor Mr Snelling. The moment she heard that Mendax had run away, she had begun to wail.

"I'm FRIGHTENED!" she wailed now. "This is magic, and we've got the Power Hat so magic isn't supposed to hurt us! Oh, Skirty, perhaps Mrs Abercrombie's horrible SQUASHED GHOST has come out of her tunnel and STOLEN Mendax!"

"Rubbish!" snapped Skirty Marm. "Pull yourself together!" She was stern because she was secretly frightened herself. This was certainly the work of magic – but *who* or *what* could force Mendax to run away, now that Mrs Abercrombie was dead?

"I miss him so much!" sniffed the vicar. "Witches, I can feel that my little cat is in dreadful *danger* – and I must face that danger with him! Don't take any notice of the letter. I want you to cast a finding spell right away!"

Old Noshie and Skirty Marm exchanged uneasy looks. They hated to disappoint Mr Snelling, and they did not want to make him any more worried, but it had to be said.

Skirty Marm spoke as gently as she could.

"It's not as simple as that, I'm afraid. The whole point of the finding spell is to find things that are LOST – and Mendax isn't lost."

"Not lost!" the vicar cried indignantly. "Of course he is! Don't tell me that spell won't work!"

"I quote," said Skirty Marm, "Red-Stocking Spellbook, Chapter two thousand and ninety, page one hundred and eleven thousand. Part A, subsection B. 'Any object that has left a place on purpose, willingly and of its own accord, and then knows where it is when it has got there, SHALL NOT BE DEEMED LOST FOR PURPOSES OF THIS SPELL.'" She added, "I had to write that out two thousand times for a punishment at school."

Mr Snelling's face fell. He did not understand this, but it sounded very legal and definite.

Old Noshie kindly patted his shoulder. "I'm sorry. We'd find him if we could – wouldn't we?"

"Oh, yes," Skirty Marm said. "I haven't always seen eye to eye with that cat, but it won't be the same village without him."

"I'll make you a nice cup of tea," said Alice. "Then you can have a rest, to get over the shock. Cuthbert and I will carry on arranging the Harvest Supper."

Mr Snelling shook his head forlornly and stood up. "Mendax wouldn't want me to mope. He'd expect me to carry on. I don't want to let him down."

The vicar was as good as his word and went on with his work in the same old way. But his unhappy face made everyone very sad.

In a few hours, the news that Mendax had left was all round the village. The people of Tranters End were sorry to lose the little talking cat – but they were even sorrier for their vicar.

The next day was a Sunday. The villagers came to church as usual. It seemed very empty without the familiar figure of Mendax bustling about. Normally he was sitting on the pile of hymnbooks at the door, ready to chat to people as they came in. It was hard to look at his empty cushion, though everyone tried to be cheerful for poor Mr Snelling's sake.

Mendax usually took the collection, carrying the plate carefully between his paws. Today, Mr Noggs the churchwarden carried the plate instead, and several people sniffed as they dropped in their money.

Thomas would not lie quietly in his buggy. He moaned, "Where's Mendax? He promised to tell me a story!" Alice tried picking him up and rocking him in her arms, but still he shouted, in Babyspeak, "I want Mendax!"

When it came to the sermon, Mr Snelling plodded up the pulpit steps as if he had the world on his shoulders.

"You will all know by now," he said, in a choking voice, "that I have lost my little cat. I didn't have the heart to write my own sermon – and they're very boring, anyway. So I've brought Mendax's classic one about the Good Samaritan."

He read it out very shakily and nearly broke

down twice. Altogether, it was a sad service. Afterwards, everyone tried to think of something comforting to say to the vicar.

Mrs Brightpie patted his arm gently. "Now, Mr Snelling, you're not to fret. Mendax is a very clever cat. I'm sure he can take care of himself. And cats aren't like us humans, you know – they don't feel things as deeply."

"Mendax does," Mr Snelling said. "He has the kindest heart in the world!"

"You mustn't lose hope," soothed Mrs Brightpie. "Why, he might come strolling back any minute!"

"I wish he would!" sniffed Old Noshie as she followed Skirty Marm back up the one hundred and eighty-six steps to the belfry. "Oh, Skirt, nothing's right without Mendax!"

Skirty Marm had been frowning a lot ever since she had read Mendax's letter. It was her thinking frown, which showed her clever brain was working hard.

"I just wish I knew what made him so scared that he had to run away! If it is something to do with magic, why didn't he leave a message for us?"

4

The Warning of the Ants

Mr Babbercorn had suggested cancelling the Harvest Supper because of Mendax's disappearance. The vicar, however, would not hear of it.

"Mendax did a lot of work for this Harvest Supper – why, he left a bag of sponge cakes in the freezer specially! If we didn't have it, we'd be letting him down."

Mrs Brightpie said the vicar was very brave. And despite having a bad leg and not being very strong, she insisted on helping with the arrangements. Thanks to her, the Harvest Supper was a splendid affair. Sad as they were about Mendax, the people of Tranters End could not help gasping with delight when they filed into the village hall.

"Wow!" cried Old Noshie. "Look at the GRUB!"

41

Mrs Brightpie had tried to cheer things up by decorating the hall with branches of apples, bunches of grapes and coloured paper lanterns. The long tables were groaning with food. As well as the things the villagers had given, Mrs Brightpie had paid for huge bowls of delicious trifle, jellies in every colour of the rainbow and plates of sweets for the children.

"Bless her!" whispered Alice, with tears in her eyes. "She won't let us miss him too much!"

It was hard not to have a good time when Mrs Brightpie herself sat down at the piano and played country dances. Old Noshie and Skirty Marm loved to dance, and they jumped and pranced like two whirling dervishes. They were wearing their new Brownie uniforms in public for the first time, which greatly added to their enjoyment.

"If only Mendax hadn't run away," Skirty Marm said, "this would be PERFECT!"

Thomas was still cross and grizzly. Alice had parked his buggy in the little kitchen that opened off the hall, but this only made him worse. About halfway through the supper he broke into roars, and Alice had to shut the door so nobody would hear him. She rocked him and jiggled him and sang his favourite songs. And still he bellowed.

The music was loud, and the witches did not hear Thomas until they stopped for a rest. Skirty Marm, who had very sharp ears, suddenly grabbed Old Noshie by the sleeve of her Brownie shirt.

"Listen! He's calling US!"

Sure enough, over the jolly strains of "Strip the Willow", they heard Thomas's voice: "Noshie! Skirty! HELP!"

They rushed out to the kitchen.

"AT LAST!" yelled Thomas, in Babyspeak. And he stopped crying.

"Thank goodness!" gasped Alice. "I don't know what's the matter with him tonight!"

"Send her away," ordered Thomas. "I have to talk to you *in private*!"

The witches knew there was no point saying this to Alice – she still refused to believe that they could understand her baby.

"Poor Alice, you haven't had any supper," said Skirty Marm. "You go and have something to eat – we'll take care of Thomas."

Alice was rather puzzled, but too relieved to

get away from her squealing baby to ask any questions.

"Thanks, witches. I'll only be a minute." She paused on her way out of the kitchen. "This place is full of ants, and they keep trying to climb on the buggy. Do keep them away from Thomas."

The damp little kitchen was swarming with tiny black ants. A line of them were marching up the handle of Thomas's buggy.

"Shoo!" said Old Noshie. "Pesky things!" She had brought a plate of flapjacks and did not intend to share them with a lot of greedy ants.

"Leave them alone!" cried Thomas. "They've come with a WARNING!"

Skirty Marm sat down beside him. "All right, what's all this about?"

"It's Mrs Brightpie!" Thomas said. "You have to make her go away!"

"Go away? Certainly not!" said Skirty Marm. "She's turned this Harvest Supper into the brilliantest party ever – and she got us these smart Brownie uniforms!"

"She said I was the best dancer in the village," Old Noshie added proudly.

"You don't understand!" moaned Thomas.

"The ants told me she's DANGEROUS and HORRIBLE!"

Old Noshie and Skirty Marm burst out laughing.

"What, Mrs Brightpie?" Old Noshie took a big bite of her flapjack, which the kind lady had provided. "She's a WONDERFUL human!"

"She's a WITCH!" Thomas cried. "The ants recognized her!"

Skirty Marm looked sternly at the ants. "What do they know about anything? And what have they got against witches? They'll be telling US to go away next!"

"Cheek!" said Old Noshie, with her mouth full.

Skirty Marm patted Thomas's velvety bald head. "Now, Thomas," she said, in a kind-but-firm voice copied from Mr Babbercorn, "when we gave you that lovely present, we didn't expect you to believe any old rubbish the animals told you! Ants are well-known troublemakers. They'll do anything to get at human food."

The ants began to mill about on the buggy and on the floor, as if they were angry.

"They're just jealous of our lovely party," Old

45

Noshie said comfortably. "Back home on Witch Island, we eat ants."

"Don't you eat any of these!" Thomas screamed, kicking his short legs furiously. "They're my FRIENDS!"

"Keep your hair on," said Skirty Marm. "I mean, keep your fuzz on. This sort of thing is typical ant behaviour. You're very tired from all that yelling, so I'm going to cast one of my sleep spells. And you're not to worry."

She muttered her sleep spell. Thomas, in the middle of his fury, suddenly yawned and smiled. Before Skirty had finished, he was fast asleep.

"You'll be in trouble, if Alice finds out about that spell," said Old Noshie. "Cor, doesn't he make a lot of noise for such a little person?"

"What a load of old RUBBISH about Mrs Brightpie!" exclaimed Skirty Marm. She stamped her foot crossly at the scurrying ants. "Get out of this kitchen!"

At that moment, the door opened and in came Mrs Brightpie herself. She was carrying a tray of dirty plates, and she gave the witches one of her sweet smiles. It was very hard indeed to believe that this kind lady – who had given them their treasured Brownie uniforms – was wicked or dangerous.

"You clever things, you've got poor little Thomas off to sleep!" she said. "I wonder what was the matter with him?"

Old Noshie happened to be standing beside the sink, which was full of water. In the second before Mrs Brightpie dropped in the plates, Old Noshie saw something reflected on the smooth surface of the water – something that turned her green skin the colour of a raw sprout.

Where she should have seen the pretty face of Mrs Brightpie, she saw a hideous, HAIRY FACE. Where she should have seen Mrs Brightpie's charming smile, she saw a deadly row of METAL TEETH.

It was the face that haunted her worst nightmares – the kind of nightmares she got after eating human cheese, which never agreed with her.

She stood with her mouth hanging open and her eyes like saucers.

"What's up with you?" asked Skirty Marm after Mrs Brightpie had left the kitchen.

At first, Old Noshie could only make a strange grunting noise. "Huuurrrrr . . ."

Skirty Marm took off her friend's pointed hat and blue wig, and gave her bald head a brisk whack with a teacup.

"It's for your own good, Nosh. Now tell me what's the matter – you look like you've seen a ghost!"

"I HAVE!" croaked Old Noshie. "I saw MRS ABERCROMBIE! It was meant to be Mrs Brightpie's reflection – but it was HERS!"

Skirty Marm was frightened. "Don't YOU start!" she yelled.

"I did, Skirt – honest I did! And you know what that means!"

"When a witch wants to disguise herself," Skirty Marm said, "she can take on any shape – but she can't disguise her REFLECTION. Of course I know that – it was one of our first lessons! But Mrs Brightpie's not like that. She's not evil or ugly – and anyway, someone would have noticed by now. How could she go to the hairdressers if she couldn't show her reflection?"

There was a terrible chilly feeling in the pit of Skirty Marm's stomach. She knew Old Noshie was telling the truth, but she still did not want to believe it.

"Anyway, that's not a proper reflection," she blustered. "That's just scummy washing-up water! Let's get back into the hall and look at her proper reflection in a window or something. Then you'll see this is STUPID!"

"I don't dare," quavered Old Noshie. "Oh, Skirty, what are we going to do? She didn't die in that tunnel after all! And now she's come here to snatch back the Power Hat – and we'll be KILLED!"

Before Skirty Marm could reply, Alice came back into the kitchen. "Oh, how wonderful – Thomas is asleep! Thank you for looking after him, witches."

She was slightly surprised when Skirty Marm grabbed Old Noshie by the arm and dragged her out of the room without a word.

In the hall, the Harvest Supper was in full swing. The village children played games under the long tables, eating the sweets Mrs Brightpie had given them. The grown-ups sat with cups of tea or danced to the loud music that boomed from Mrs Tucker's tape-deck.

Mrs Brightpie could not dance because of her bad leg. She sat beside the vicar, and you could see from the expression on her face that she was saying comforting things about Mendax. It really was extremely difficult to believe that this kind lady had anything to do with the dreadful Mrs Abercrombie.

Skirty Marm heaved a shaky sigh of relief. "You really got me going that time, you old IDIOT!" she snapped. "We'll find her reflection, and then you'll see that you're BONKERS!"

She looked around the hall, so beautifully decorated for the Harvest Supper – and saw that every single window had been covered with sheaves of corn or huge bunches of leaves. Not a single thing on any of the tables was shiny enough to reflect anything. Even the spoons were made of dull white plastic.

Skirty Marm breathed gently on the palm of her hand, and her lips moved with the words of a spell. Her palm began to shine as if someone had covered it with a sheet of mercury. Very quickly, making super-sure nobody but Noshie was watching, she tilted her gleaming silver palm towards Mrs Brightpie.

"Told you," muttered Old Noshie.

Skirty Marm could not speak. Across the room, Mrs Brightpie sat with her hand on Mr Snelling's knee. In the reflection, the innocent vicar was sitting next to the evil ugly figure of Mrs Abercrombie.

5

True Colours

At the end of the Harvest Supper, Mr Snelling made a speech thanking Mrs Brightpie for all her generosity. She stood beside the door, shaking hands with every single person as they left.

To Mr Babbercorn's annoyance, Old Noshie and Skirty Marm refused to line up for the hand-shaking. They had started to behave very oddly – whispering and trembling and trying to hide behind the hall curtains.

"I really think you should come and thank Mrs Brightpie," Mr Babbercorn told them.

"NO!" squealed the witches.

They jumped up to the ceiling like two enormous frogs, and wriggled out through the skylight.

"I'm terribly sorry," Mr Babbercorn said to Mrs Brightpie. "I can't think why they're being so rude."

"Don't worry!" laughed Mrs Brightpie, warmly shaking his hand, "Witches will be witches!"

Back at the vicarage, the increasingly exasperated curate found Old Noshie and Skirty Marm crouching under the draining-board with tea towels over their faces.

"For goodness sake!" Mr Babbercorn said, rather sharply. "What has got into you two? Why on earth did you zoom out through the roof like that?"

"Don't be too hard on them," said gentle Alice. "I think something has frightened them. Come out, witches – there's nothing to be scared of here!"

"Draw the blinds!" hissed Skirty Marm, behind her tea towel.

Mr Babbercorn and Mr Snelling sighed impatiently, but Alice drew the blinds across the kitchen windows. Only then did the witches dare to uncover their faces and crawl out.

"I've had a terrible SHOCK!" moaned Old Noshie. "I need a HUGE BISCUIT!"

"You'd better sit down, you lot," Skirty Marm said grimly. "We've got some bad news."

Pale and trembling, she told them the awful truth – that the lady they knew as Mrs Brightpie was Mrs Abercrombie in disguise.

For a long moment, there was a stunned silence. Then the three grown-up humans burst out *laughing* – even Mr Snelling, who had not so much as smiled since the disappearance of Mendax. They laughed and laughed. The bare idea of delightful Mrs Brightpie secretly being the evil Mrs Abercrombie was too hilarious for words.

"Oh, you ridiculous witches!" cried Mr Snelling. "What will you think of next?"

"They don't believe us!" wailed Old Noshie.

Skirty Marm stamped her foot. "You fools!" she shouted. "Why won't you listen to us? Don't you care that we're in DANGER?"

Mr Babbercorn wiped the tears of laughter from his glasses.

"Of course we care," he said. "But you're not in danger! Mrs Brightpie wouldn't hurt a fly!"

"No – she'd be too busy EATING them!" growled Skirty Marm.

"We've seen Mrs Abercrombie, so we know what she looks like," Mr Snelling pointed out. He shuddered. "She's huge and hideous – and dear Mrs Brightpie is very nice-looking, I always think." He cleared his throat and blushed slightly. "She told me her first name is 'Petunia'. I think it suits her."

"It's all a trick!" Skirty Marm raged. "She had us fooled too! She was asking us very sneaky questions about the Power Hat – thank goodness we didn't tell her where it was!"

"Or we'd be DEAD," Old Noshie put in solemnly.

"I tell you, that woman is a desperate witch!" cried Skirty Marm. "We have to BURN her immediately!"

"Oh, do be reasonable," sighed Mr Snelling. "How can we burn a respectable lady like Mrs Brightpie? This is nonsense!"

"You're just over-excited," Alice said kindly. "When you've had a good night's sleep, you'll realize you're being silly."

"Don't you see?" Skirty Marm cried. "This must be why Mendax ran away! He must have seen her reflection in something and lost his nerve!"

The mention of Mendax made everyone very serious.

"My Mendax is not a coward," Mr Snelling said proudly. "He'd never run away because he was scared. Really, witches – let's have an end to this at once! I won't have poor Mrs Brightpie insulted! Certainly not when she's given all that money to the organ fund."

Skirty Marm spoke bitterly. "Yes, she BOUGHT you. Just like she BOUGHT me and Nosh with these Brownie uniforms. Come on, Noshie. Let's go home and take them off!"

The two witches left the vicarage without saying goodnight. They climbed up the one hundred and eighty-six belfry steps and changed back into their witchy rags. Then Skirty Marm dragged her cushion over to her favourite thinking place, under the larger of the two great bells.

Old Noshie plumped down beside her. "What do we do now, Skirt?" she asked in a small, worried voice.

"Nothing," said Skirty Marm grimly, "except WAIT. She'll reveal herself to us when she's ready. And I mean to be ready too!"

Deep in the woods, hidden by a thick grove of trees, a light burned in the window of Mrs Brightpie's cottage. The people of Tranters End – who had had such a splendid time at the Harvest Supper – would have been astonished at the scene in the kitchen.

An iron cauldron was bubbling over a large fire. Mrs Brightpie, no longer smiling, was pacing up and down impatiently. A rusty iron cage hung beside the window. Inside it was the huddled form of Mendax. He did not look sleek or elegant now. One of his ears was bent, his whiskers drooped and he was shaking like a leaf.

His green eyes were fixed fearfully on the third creature in the room. At the table sat a very dirty old witch, with only one black tooth and filthy grey hair. She was chewing her way through a huge plate of deep-fried mice (and very horrible it sounded when she crunched them in her gums). Every now and then, this toothless old witch took a swig from a large brown bottle of Nasty Medicine. As all sensible humans know, it is very STUPID and DANGEROUS to drink someone else's medicine, but witches regard it as a treat.

And this old witch certainly loved it. Mendax shuddered as he remembered her drunken rages. Seeing her was like seeing his worst nightmare for she was none other than Mrs Wilkins, the coarse and low-class witch who had once owned him. And although the cat-slaves were now free, Mrs Wilkins still had power over him – because she knew his code.

I should explain that, in the bad old days, every cat-slave had a code (rather like the number on a credit card) known only to his owner. This meant that no cat could have a secret – his owner could always activate the code and get it out of him. Mendax had run away from the vicarage when he spotted Mrs Brightpie's horrible reflection in a puddle and realized that if she got his code he would not be able to help giving away the secret of the Power Hat. He hadn't had time to warn the witches.

"Get on with it!" shouted Mrs Brightpie crossly. "I warn you, Mrs Wilkins – my patience is running out!"

"I'm still hungry," mumbled Mrs Wilkins. "They starved us in that prison. And I sold all me teeth to buy Medicine, so eating takes me a while these days."

After the defeat of the queen, Mrs Wilkins had done a stretch in prison for cruelty to cat-slaves.

"Hurry up!" snapped Mrs Brightpie. She whacked Mendax's cage with her stick. "I'm paying you for this cat's CODE! Once I've got it, he'll have to tell me where they hid my Power Hat!"

"Using cat-codes is against the law on Witch Island now," said Mrs Wilkins. "If I get found out, I'll go straight back to prison. You'd better kill him when you've finished, in case he reports us."

"Mind your own business!" stormed the former queen. "And finish that food! I want my Power Hat before morning – and before those two interfering Red-Stockings find out I've got Mendax!"

"Good thing you caught him so quickly," Mrs Wilkins remarked. A mouse's tail hung from her lower lip. She sucked it in like a strand of spaghetti. "You want to watch him. He's *slippery*, that one."

"He won't be able to lie when you've given me his code," said Mrs Brightpie.

Inside the cage, Mendax groaned.

Mrs Brightpie ignored the heart-rending sound. "This human disguise is very hard work," she said. "While you're guzzling, I'll change into something more comfortable."

Before the horrified eyes of Mendax, her pretty white curls changed to greasy snakes of grey. Her teeth turned to metal. A rough beard sprouted on her chin. She swelled and grew until her head brushed the ceiling. Her neat blue dress changed to musty, dusty black rags.

Mrs Abercrombie, ex-queen of Witch Island, was herself again. The sight was so ugly that Mendax had to stuff a paw in his mouth to hold back a scream.

"Cor, that's better!" said Mrs Wilkins. "You didn't half look sickening in that disguise!"

Her plate was nearly empty. Mendax had served her many meals in the miserable past and recognized the signs that she was getting tired of eating. Any minute now, his secrets would be torn from him like a cork being pulled out of a bottle.

"Mrs Abercrombie will grab the Power Hat and make it do UNSPEAKABLE things," Mendax whispered sadly to himself. "Noshie and Skirty will be killed – I'll probably end up in some illegal Cat Pie—"

He stopped suddenly. A small brown spider was scurrying across the windowsill beside him. Mendax remembered the magic christening gift.

Without moving a whisker he whispered, "Listen, spider – this is an EMERGENCY! Get a message to the baby at the vicarage. Tell him to tell the witches – SAVE THE HAT!"

Old Noshie and Skirty Marm had fallen asleep on the belfry floor – Old Noshie pointlessly clutching a brick to use as a weapon in case Mrs Abercrombie appeared. At the dead of night, when the moon was high and the village was cloaked in darkness, they were woken up by the screams of Thomas. Distantly, they heard him yelling.

"Witches – message from Mendax! Come quickly!"

Skirty Marm was the first to wake up properly. She leapt to her feet.

"Come on, Nosh – Thomas wants us!"

Old Noshie scrambled up, rubbing her sleepy eyes, and dropped the brick on her foot. "OW!"

The two of them rushed down the one hundred and eighty-six belfry steps and hurried across the dark garden to the vicarage. There, they found the vicar, Mr Babbercorn and Alice desperately trying to comfort a shrieking baby.

Alice was almost crying. "Oh witches, can

you do anything? He's been screaming for hours, and I don't know what's the matter!"

"ABOUT TIME!" yelled Thomas, in Babyspeak.

"Sorry, Thomas," said Old Noshie. "What's the message?"

"Mrs Abercrombie has got Mendax!" Thomas cried. "He says SAVE THE HAT before she breaks his code!"

"Who told you?" demanded Skirty Marm. "Are you sure it's not one of his lies?"

"Mendax told a spider, who told a bird," Thomas said. "The bird tapped his beak on the window and told me. And I had to scream until you heard."

"Nice work!" said Old Noshie, patting his bald head. "You can go back to sleep now."

And to the amazement of his exhausted parents, Thomas fell asleep. It was as if someone had switched off a radio.

"I don't understand!" said Alice when they were all standing in the kitchen. "What is going on?"

"Ummm . . ." said Old Noshie.

"Err . . ." said Skirty Marm.

They didn't dare tell Mr Babbercorn and Alice

that they had been casting spells on the baby. They knew Mr Babbercorn would be very cross with them. Skirty Marm gave Old Noshie a hard stare which meant, "Shut up and leave this to me".

"If you understood Babyspeak," she said slowly, "you'd know that Mrs Brightpie—"

"Right, that's enough!" interrupted Mr Babbercorn. It was the middle of the night, and he was very tired. This made him less patient than usual. "I don't want to hear *one more word* about poor Mrs Brightpie being Mrs Abercrombie in disguise. Mrs Abercrombie is dead. This is a lot of NONSENSE!"

"She's not dead!" cried Old Noshie. "We've got to get the— OW!"

Skirty Marm had cut her off by slapping her with a tea towel. "You'll be sorry you didn't believe us," she said darkly. "Come on, Nosh – let's not waste any more time with these silly humans!"

She grabbed Old Noshie by her ragged dress and pulled her out through the back door.

"You're barmy!" grumbled Old Noshie, out in the dark vicarage garden. "Why didn't you fetch the Power Hat?"

64

"Mr B. wouldn't have let us," snapped Skirty Marm. "We'll have to SNEAK it away, without him knowing."

"But HOW, Skirt?"

The Power Hat, disguised as a knitted bobble hat, was hidden in Mr Babbercorn's underwear drawer. This was the safe place they had chosen for it the last time Mrs Abercrombie had tried to steal it back. Mr Babbercorn had almost forgotten it was there – though it kept his vests and pants in such perfect condition that they never wore out.

Skirty Marm was scornful. "You really are a very THICK WITCH, Noshie. Don't you remember the spell we learned at school, in the 37th form?"

"I've forgotten," Old Noshie said. "I must have been eating my packed lunch."

"We're going to make ourselves INVISIBLE," Skirty Marm said sternly. "Put your wig on straight and repeat after me . . ."

Skirty Marm had a very good memory, but she did not have her Red-Stocking Spellbook. When the Invisibility Spell was complete, both witches shrieked. They had disappeared – but their clothes had not. The invisible Old Noshie looked especially strange, with her pointed hat and lopsided blue wig hanging in mid-air above her ragged dress.

"Drat," muttered Skirty Marm. "I must have left something out!"

"Let's try again," suggested Old Noshie.

Skirty Marm shook her head – her friend could tell by the way her empty hat wobbled in the air. "There's no time. Mrs A. could be here any minute to grab the hat! Don't you see? Mendax sent the message because he knew Mrs A. had his CODE! We'll just have to take all our clothes off."

"What?" gasped Old Noshie. "And go creeping round the vicarage IN THE NUDE? Are you MAD?"

Skirty Marm's clothes were already dropping in a crumpled heap on the lawn. "They won't be able to SEE us – that's the whole point! Now, hurry up and take your clothes off."

Old Noshie did not like it, but she always did as she was told in the end. Her clothes joined the heap. Both witches were now totally invisible.

"BRRR!" grumbled the voice of Old Noshie, eerie in the darkness. "I've got goose-pimples the size of acorns!"

"Shhh!" hissed the voice of Skirty Marm.

"Where are you, Skirt?"

"In the bushes." Skirty Marm rustled the laurel bushes to show Old Noshie where she was.

In chilly, naked silence, the two witches waited for the lights to go out in the vicarage. When the house was dark and quiet, they tiptoed across the lawn.

"Hang on – what's this?" Skirty Marm snatched at a strange shape bobbing through the air beside her. "You old fool – you forgot to take off your WIG!"

"Give it back, smelly!" growled Old Noshie. "It's all right for you – you've got HAIR! My head's freezing!"

Skirty Marm threw the blue wig across the garden. Old Noshie tried to smack Skirty Marm, but could not find her. She spat on Skirty's clothes instead. Skirty Marm squashed Old Noshie's pointed hat.

"This is stupid!" she whispered crossly. "We haven't got time to fight! The minute she gets that cat's code, we're sunk!"

"All right," muttered Old Noshie. "I'll biff you when I can see you."

The invisible witches climbed into the vicarage through the bathroom window. They crept into the hall – and got a shock when they came face to face with their nude reflections in the big mirror (very few spells can fool a mirror).

Somewhere above them, they could hear the snores of Mr Snelling. They scurried up the stairs. Very careful not to tread on any creaking floorboards, they tiptoed into the curate's bedroom.

Mr Babbercorn and Alice lay fast asleep in the big double bed. Thomas lay fast asleep in his cot. Slowly – a centimetre at a time – the witches pulled open the drawer where Mr Babbercorn kept his underwear.

Skirty Marm rummaged inside it and whisked out the Power Hat in its disguise as a black-and-white bobble hat. She rammed it on her invisible head. She had worn the Power Hat before and did not enjoy it. The Hat did not weigh much when you held it in your hand, but it lay upon the brain like a ton of lead.

As long as Skirty Marm was wearing it, however, the witches were safe. Their teeth chattering with cold, they left the house, picked

up their clothes from the garden and rushed up
the one hundred and eighty-six steps to the
belfry. Skirty Marm reversed the spell to make
them visible again, and they heaved deep sighs
of relief as they scrambled into their clothes. Old
Noshie, who hated being invisible, kept looking
affectionately at her hands and trying to squint
over her shoulder to check that her bottom was
still there.

"Mrs A. can't hurt us now!" she said.

"Maybe not!" snarled a terrible voice. "But I
can hurt MENDAX!"

There was a blinding flash of lightning, and the witches screamed in terror. Mrs Abercrombie, her metal teeth gleaming wickedly, was in their belfry.

6

The Helpful Hat

"I've been PATIENT!" roared Mrs Abercrombie. "I've watched you two, waiting for you to lead me to the Hat! And I was TOO LATE! Drat and double-drat! By the time that cat told me where it was, there was nothing in the drawer but UNDERWEAR! So it's time to face you IN PERSON!"

Old Noshie bravely picked up her brick and hurled it at Mrs Abercrombie's face. The former queen caught it in her mouth, crunched it up like a gingernut and swallowed it. Then she licked her lips and smiled horribly.

"I've been looking forward to this – I bet you're THRILLED to see me!"

Skirty Marm stood up as straight as she could and folded her arms to hide their trembling.

"We've been expecting you," she said. "And you're wasting your time. The Power Hat is on my head – and that's where it's STAYING."

Mrs Abercrombie's sudden scowl of fury was a terrible thing to see. Old Noshie ran behind Skirty Marm and peeped over her shoulder.

"I missed it!" Mrs Abercrombie shrieked. "It was nearly in my grasp – and I missed it! I'd like to know how that blasted little cat-slave managed to warn you! But it's not over yet. Your queen has come with an offer."

"You're not our queen!" shouted Skirty Marm. She stuck out her tongue, which was dark purple. "What can you do to us? POOH to your offer – and shut the door on your way out."

"Miserable Red-Stocking!" thundered the ex-queen. "Give me my Power Hat!"

"NO!" yelled Skirty Marm.

"No!" squeaked Old Noshie.

Mrs Abercrombie looked around for something to sit on. There were no chairs in the belfry, so she picked up the witches' cushions and settled herself on the floor with a loud grunt.

"Let's be reasonable," she said. "You don't know how to use my Hat. It's wasted on you. You don't understand what I've been through to get my hands on it. I used my underground cave on Witch Island to make myself piles of rubbishy human money. And when I'd made enough, I blew up the cave and let everyone think I was dead. Then I came here and had to pretend to be nice to humans. It's been very hard work."

"I suppose the State Funeral's off now," Old Noshie said, in a disappointed voice. "I was looking forward to the fireworks."

Mrs Abercrombie ignored this. Her mean little eyes stared hard at Skirty Marm. "Here's my offer. Give me back my Power Hat, and I'll allow you to live. What's more, I'll allow that skinny little cat to live too."

"If I give you the Hat, you'll destroy the peaceful, democratic government of Witch Island," said Skirty Marm. "You'll kill or imprison every witch who stands against you!"

"True," said Mrs Abercrombie. "But why should you care about that? You can stay here. We don't want your sort on Witch Island anyway – you and your filthy human ways!"

"We care about Chancellor Badsleeves and all our friends," said Skirty Marm sternly. "We'll never let you hurt them!"

"Well, that's just the sort of thing I mean," said Mrs Abercrombie. "Filthy." A shudder of disgust rippled across her huge body.

Old Noshie whispered in Skirty Marm's ear, "Ask her what will happen if we DON'T give her the Hat!"

"Your daft green pal shows a glimmer of sense for once," Mrs Abercrombie said, with a spine-chilling cackle. "What a good question! If you DON'T give me my Hat, I will EAT the cat-slave Mendax. It's your choice."

The witches stared at each other in dismay. This looked impossible. If Mrs Abercrombie ate Mendax poor Mr Snelling's heart would break.

But if they saved Mendax, by giving the Hat to Mrs Abercrombie, their friends on Witch Island would have a terrible time. Chancellor Badsleeves and her Red-Stocking government would be killed immediately, probably in some particularly horrible new way. Mrs Abercrombie was famous for thinking up new ways to kill other witches – she had written a classic book on the subject (*A Hundred Horrible Deaths*, published by Belch & Squelch at 10 Witch-shillings, please allow 28 years for delivery).

"Oh, Skirt!" quavered Old Noshie. "Whatever shall we do?"

Skirty Marm suddenly remembered she was wearing the Power Hat. She shut her eyes, and spoke to it inside her head, so Mrs Abercrombie would not hear her. "Hat – Mrs A.'s right – I don't know enough about you to use you properly. Can't you just tell me if there's anything I can do?"

Green letters appeared on the blackness inside her head – rather like the letters on an old-fashioned computer screen.

I'm not supposed to give advice, typed the Hat.

Skirty Marm sighed impatiently. "You've become a very SOPPY Hat since you turned Good! Can't you just give me a *clue*?"

I am not permitted to express political opinions, typed the Hat. *But you are right, incompetent and ignorant witch – I do hate Mrs Abercrombie and I dread doing her dirty work again! So pay attention. I shall type this only once. You must command me to give Mendax a good CLOAKING.*

"A *what*?" Skirty Marm asked, in her thoughts.

It means I cloak him in a shell of protective magic, typed the Power Hat. *She can keep the cat, but she won't be able to eat him – she won't be able to hurt him at all.*

"Just the thing!" cried Skirty, inwardly. "Hat – give Mendax a cloaking!"

Certainly. But there's a slight snag, typed the Hat. *It only lasts for one week, and it cannot be renewed. So you will have just one week to rescue your cat-friend. After that, he will be cat-fritters.*

Mrs Abercrombie suddenly leapt up and stamped her foot so hard that one of the floorboards cracked.

"Something's been CLOAKED!" she screamed, turning puce with fury. "I can feel it! Drat and double-drat – you've cloaked that pesky cat!"

"What's she talking about?" wondered Old Noshie.

"Shut your green face!" roared Mrs Abercrombie. She turned back to Skirty Marm, simmering with rage. "So – you think you're clever because you know about Advanced Cloaking! But the fight isn't over yet! This time next week, you'll be begging me ON YOUR

KNEES to take the Power Hat!"

She raised her arms – and vanished.

Her voice hung in the empty air: "Remember – one week!"

The witches were very pleased and proud to have got rid of Mrs Abercrombie, but the pleasure wore off when they realized they were no nearer to saving Mendax.

"This cloaking thing isn't much use if Mrs A.'s still got him!" sighed Old Noshie. "And we've only got a week to think of something!"

It was all the harder because their friends at the vicarage would not hear a word against Mrs Brightpie. They did not believe the witches' garbled story about cloaking Mendax in magic. They were all getting very annoyed with Old Noshie and Skirty Marm.

"For the last time," Mr Snelling said crossly, "I don't want to hear any more about Mrs Brightpie being wicked. I don't want to hear how she's got my Mendax – why, she's put a notice about him in the post office window, offering a reward to anyone who sees him! Don't tell me the late Mrs Abercrombie ever did anything as nice as that!"

Mr Babbercorn tried to be kind and

understanding. "Perhaps you're a bit jealous of Mrs Brightpie," he suggested, "because everyone likes her so much."

"JEALOUS?" gasped the witches. This was so unfair it was absolutely outrageous. It was particularly awful to be thought nasty and selfish when they were trying so hard to be brave and good.

One by one, the days slipped past. Old Noshie and Skirty Marm stayed miserably in their belfry, racking their brains for a way of saving Mendax before the cloaking spell ran out.

For this reason, they did not hear of Mrs Brightpie's latest plan – until it was too late.

The last day of the cloaking spell was Hallowe'en. For witches this is the most important night of the year, when they ride out on their broomsticks to play tricks on innocent humans. For humans, however, Hallowe'en means nothing more than fun – and the people of Tranters End were delighted when Mrs Brightpie invited every child in the village to a grand party at her new house in the woods.

"My house is full of surprises!" smiled Mrs

Brightpie. "I'd like the dear children to see it first!"

"How kind," Alice said when she heard about the party. "I wish Thomas was big enough to go – it's bound to be wonderful."

At teatime on Hallowe'en, the twenty children of Tranters End set out through the woods. They were wearing Hallowe'en costumes – the three Blenkinsops, from Blodge Farm, were particularly gruesome as vampires, with false blood dripping out of their mouths. Little Amy Noggs, dressed as a red demon with plastic horns, carried a large bunch of flowers for Mrs Brightpie. All the children were very excited and very curious to see what Mrs Brightpie had done to the woodman's cottage.

"WOW!" cried Ben Blenkinsop.

The children gaped at the cottage, sitting so prettily in its sunlit clearing.

Its walls were reddish-brown and looked soft to the touch. Emma Blenkinsop prodded it with her finger – and shrieked when her finger sank in. It looked soft because it was soft. It was soft because it was made of moist, delicious slabs of *gingerbread*.

The windows were surrounded with white

chocolate. The front door was made of dark chocolate and surrounded with a pretty pattern of Maltesers. The sloping roof was covered with green and red fruit gums. The window boxes were made of toffee and filled with liquorice-allsort flowers.

With yells of hungry delight, the children rushed up to the house and began pulling bits off.

Only Amy Noggs hung back. She watched the others stuffing themselves with cake, sweets and toffee.

"Only WICKED WITCHES have gingerbread houses!" she whispered.

Nobody heard her.

7

Panic

It was nearly dark when the parents of Tranters End trooped through the woods to collect their children from Mrs Brightpie's Hallowe'en party. They were all impatient to get a look at her famous cottage.

"I've heard she's put in a swimming pool," said Mrs Blenkinsop.

"No, no!" said Mr Noggs the churchwarden, who was Amy's grandfather. "She's built a huge conservatory!"

"Here we are," said Mrs Tucker, who was fetching her two young nephews. "Well – doesn't it look a picture?"

Deep in the forest, the grey stone walls of the cottage glowed in the last rays of the setting sun. It was as neat and quaint as a picture on a calendar with its red-tiled roof and window boxes full of geraniums.

The parents were a little distance away but they could see the dainty figure of Mrs Brightpie, waiting for them in the cottage doorway.

"Isn't it quiet?" remarked Mrs Blenkinsop. "You'd never think there was a children's party going on, would you?" She sounded uneasy. "You wouldn't catch me living out here in the middle of nowhere!"

They hurried towards Mrs Brightpie. By now, the silence seemed decidedly strange.

"Good evening, Mrs Brightpie," said Mr Noggs. "I hope the kids haven't worn you out!"

"Not at all!" smiled Mrs Brightpie.

The parents stood listening to the wind in the trees and the deepening silence. Mrs Brightpie watched them, still smiling.

After a few minutes, Mrs Tucker cleared her throat nervously.

"Where – where *are* the children?"

"I've got your children," said Mrs Brightpie.

And before their horrified eyes, a terrible change swept over her. She grew until she filled the doorway. Her eyes glinted fiendishly. Her teeth became metal daggers, and suddenly she wore the tattered black rags of a WITCH.

Several of the parents screamed. They all

knew at once that this was not a witch like Old Noshie and Skirty Marm, but a wicked witch from a nightmare.

Mr Noggs tried to sound brave.

"Give us the children and we'll say no more about this."

Mrs Abercrombie chortled. There was a flash of lightning and a mighty clap of thunder. Mrs Blenkinsop and Mrs Tucker had started to cry.

In a deep, gravelly voice, the old witch boomed, "I am MRS ABERCROMBIE, rightful queen of Witch Island! Miserable humans, you are POWERLESS before me! If you want to see your children again, you'd better bring me Old Noshie and Skirty Marm!"

In an explosion of black smoke that left everybody coughing, she vanished. Iron shutters clanged across the doors and windows of the cottage. The panic-stricken parents rushed forward, banging on doors and thumping on windows. They screamed the children's names, they begged Mrs Abercrombie to take pity on them.

It was useless. Though they hated to leave their children, there was only one thing to do.

They rushed through the shadowy forest to the vicarage.

"Good gracious!" choked Mr Snelling when he heard the awful news. "The witches were right all along! Besides our children, that ghastly Mrs Abercrombie has got my Mendax! Oh, what on earth are we going to do?"

"We tried to warn you about that Mrs Brightpie," Old Noshie could not help saying. "Well, it's too late now."

Mrs Blenkinsop began to cry again.

"Shut up, Nosh," said Skirty Marm. "You're making them depressed."

The frantic parents of Tranters End were jammed into the vicarage sitting-room. Old Noshie and Skirty Marm felt dreadfully sorry for them. They were sitting on top of the piano because the room was so full. PC Bloater sat on the piano-stool taking notes – but nobody really thought there was anything the police could do.

"Look, I don't understand this stuff about a Hat," growled Mr Noggs. "And I don't care! If that's what Mrs Abercrombie wants – let her have it! All I want is my Amy!"

There were murmurs of agreement from the other parents. Old Noshie and Skirty Marm were very worried. These humans were in no mood to hear excuses about Witch Island politics. What did they care about witches' democracy when their children had been stolen?

Mr Snelling held up his hand for quiet. "If we give Mrs Abercrombie the Power Hat," he said tearfully, "we'll be putting Mendax and the witches in *terrible danger*."

"Our children are in terrible danger already!" cried Mrs Blenkinsop. "There isn't any choice!"

"But we can't trust the word of that dreadful witch," argued Mr Babbercorn. "What if she gets the Hat – and keeps the children?"

"Skirty Marm," Alice said, "can't the Power Hat help us?"

Skirty Marm shook her head. The bobble on the disguised Power Hat wobbled forlornly.

"It's all a question of knowing how to use the Hat," she explained. "I have to give it a proper COMMAND – and that would take a gigantic lot of magic."

"Maybe you're depending too much on the Hat," Mr Babbercorn said. "You're intelligent witches – there must be something you can do without it!"

Old Noshie sighed. "Two witches can't do anything against Mrs A. – not when they don't know how to work the Hat!"

"Yes," said Mr Babbercorn excitedly, "but what about more than two witches? What about FIFTY?"

"Eh?" gasped Old Noshie and Skirty Marm.

"Ask your FRIENDS for help!" Mr Babbercorn cried. "They surely don't want Mrs Abercrombie to be their queen again?"

Skirty Marm leapt off the piano as if someone had given her an electric shock.

"You're right! Our old pals from the Island will help us!"

"We must hurry," said Old Noshie, scrambling down clumsily. "Today's Hallowe'en, don't forget! They'll be taking off on their broomsticks soon, to go and bother the humans!"

"But we can't spare any time!" cried Mrs Tucker.

Alice patted her shoulder kindly. "Please give the witches a chance. If we'd listened to them in the first place, this would never have happened."

Old Noshie and Skirty Marm were already hurrying through the dark garden towards the shed. Mendax had hidden a secret radio to Witch Island here during his spying days. He had stopped being a spy ages ago, but he still used the radio to keep in contact with his cat-friends at home.

Skirty Marm lit the end of her finger for light (witches can do this easily, without hurting themselves) and held the little cat-sized headphones against one ear.

"Come in, Witch Island! Skirty Marm calling Witch Island! Mayday! Mayday!"

Over the radio came a crackling voice.

"Witch Island here. Come in, Skirty Marm."

It took Skirty several minutes of long-distance

argument before she was put in touch with Chancellor Badsleeves. The Chancellor had been democratically elected after the downfall of the queen and she was now the most important witch on the island. Luckily, she had once had the next-door cave to Old Noshie and Skirty Marm, and she was not a witch to forget old friends.

"Hello, you two!" Badsleeves called cheerfully over the radio. "Happy Hallowe'en!"

As quickly as she could, Skirty Marm told Badsleeves about the terrible situation in Tranters End.

"We need your help to save the children!"

There was a pause.

"Of course, I'd *like* to help," said Badsleeves slowly. "But it's Hallowe'en! We're supposed to be out *annoying* the humans, not *rescuing* them! The other witches aren't going to like this one bit – I'll never get it past them!"

"You dratted politicians, you're all the same!" shouted Skirty Marm. "All you care about is VOTES! Well, you listen to me, Badsleeves – if you don't help, we'll have to give Mrs A. the Power Hat! And once she gets her hands on it, you'll lose a lot more than votes!"

"For instance, HEADS," put in Old Noshie.

"The question is," Skirty Marm said sternly, "do you want Mrs A. to be your queen again?"

There was a long, thoughtful silence.

"Leave it to me," said Badsleeves.

One hour later – to the amazement of the villagers – there was a hand-picked flying broom squadron camped on the vicarage lawn. Chancellor Badsleeves and fifty of her finest witches sat in groups around five camp fires. The flickering flames made their tattered black figures look very sinister. Though the people of Tranters End knew they had come to help, they could not help being nervous. Alice shivered and held baby Thomas very tight. Could these witches rescue the children?

Mr Babbercorn bravely shook hands with Chancellor Badsleeves – he recognized her from a photograph Noshie and Skirty had loyally hung in their belfry. She was a stout, stumpy witch with short white hair and round glasses.

"This is very kind of you," he said.

"Well, it was hard to give up our Hallowe'en," said Badsleeves. "But this is our battle too. Don't worry, we'll get your little humans back."

"Do it NOW!" called Mr Noggs. "I want my Amy!"

"Patience, human!" Badsleeves said, not unkindly. "We need to plan our attack. And this is an army that flies on its stomach. We need something to eat!"

At last, the anxious people of Tranters End had something definite to do. They hurried back to their houses to gather food for fifty-one hungry witches. It was an odd mixture. PC Bloater brought some dead mice from the mouse-trap at the police station. Mrs Tucker brought a large trifle. Mrs Blenkinsop brought two packets of Weetabix, and Alice filled an old tin bath with gallons of butterscotch Instant Whip.

Badsleeves and her flying squad had never eaten human food before, but they gobbled up everything they were offered. They particularly liked the Instant Whip and the conkers brought by Mr Noggs.

Mr Babbercorn and Mr Snelling went from campfire to campfire, carrying buckets of heated water from the muddy village pond.

"Cor, that hits the spot!" said Badsleeves, licking her lips. "You've certainly taught them how to make a proper cup of witch tea!"

Old Noshie stared at a huddled, dusty figure, sitting apart from the others. "What's Mouldypage doing here?"

Mouldypage was the ancient keeper of the Witch Island State Library. She was a brilliant scholar and the only witch as old and clever as Mrs Abercrombie – they had been at school together. Mouldypage had helped the humans once before, but she was an eccentric witch and you could never predict what side she would be on.

"Has she come to help?" Skirty Marm asked hopefully.

"I don't know," admitted Badsleeves. "She just insisted on coming along. Every time I ask her what she's up to, she tells me to mind my own business."

The three witches watched, as PC Bloater approached Mouldypage with a tray of refreshments.

"Would you like a mouse – er – Madam?"

"Ah," croaked Mouldypage, "you must be the local centurion."

"What's she talking about?" asked Old Noshie.

"She hasn't visited this land since the Romans were in charge," explained Badsleeves. "She doesn't realize times have changed."

She popped a chocolate biscuit into her mouth, burped loudly and shouted, "Gather round, flying squad! Gather round, humans! Here's the PLAN!"

8

Ambush

Mrs Abercrombie opened the cellar door. Huffing and puffing, she stomped down hundreds and hundreds of stone steps. Beneath the cottage she had dug out a huge underground cave. It was chilly and damp and lit only by eerie, greenish, magical lights.

The children of Tranters End were sitting in a frightened huddle against the slimy wall. They had been thrown into the cave as soon as they arrived for the party. Little Amy Noggs was crying, and Emma Blenkinsop had her arm around her.

"Stop that noise," said Mrs Abercrombie. "I've come to tell you what's happening. If Old Noshie and Skirty Marm give me my Power Hat, you're all free. And if they don't – well, I eat you all. Us OLDER witches still enjoy eating a nice, plump human child."

"This is the worst Hallowe'en party I've ever been to," said Ben Blenkinsop.

"Well, it'll teach you not to go near ginger-bread houses," said Mrs Abercrombie, "you greedy little pigs!"

"You'll be arrested for this!" shouted Ben bravely.

"There's nothing to worry about," said Mrs Abercrombie. "As long as your parents love you enough to get my Hat."

"Of course they love us enough!" yelled Danny, the oldest Blenkinsop child. "And they HATE you! You'll be sorry when my mum gets hold of you!"

Mrs Abercrombie looked down at the alarm clock that was tied to her wrist with string. "Ah, that cloaking spell has nearly worn off. Supper-time!"

Laughing horribly, she vanished in a cloud of smelly purple smoke.

She had very much enjoyed frightening the children (though she wished more of them had been crying) and was in a jaunty mood when she appeared, in another puff of smoke, in her kitchen.

"Five minutes, cat!" she chortled, twanging

the bars of Mendax's cage. "And then you'll be in my cauldron!"

Poor Mendax had resigned himself to being eaten. He sighed. "I don't suppose I could make a suggestion about how to serve me? I'm too skinny to roast nicely, but if I'm done slowly in a casserole—"

"SILENCE!" thundered Mrs Abercrombie. "How dare you take that insolent tone with your QUEEN?"

"I'd like to point out," said Mendax, "that at the moment, you're not my queen – or anybody else's."

"I'm as good as crowned already!" snapped Mrs Abercrombie. "I've finally won back my Power Hat!"

Suddenly, a loud voice outside cried, "We've got you SURROUNDED! Come out with your hands up!"

It was Badsleeves, shouting through a megaphone she had borrowed from PC Bloater.

"NEVER!" screamed Mrs Abercrombie. "You can't do anything to ME!"

She looked wildly round the kitchen and kicked Mrs Wilkins, who was snoring beside the fire.

"Wake up! We're surrounded – and you've got to fight!"

"I'm not being paid for no fighting," grumbled Mrs Wilkins.

"You'll go straight back to prison if they catch you!" shouted Mrs Abercrombie.

"Best place for her, in my opinion," said Mendax.

Mrs Abercrombie gave his cage a brutal shove, which knocked him off his four paws. "I'll deal with you later, cat-slave!"

It was all over in a moment.

There were witches on super-powered broomsticks in every tree around the cottage. Two witches waited on the roof, ready to leap down the chimney. The humans were on the ground, armed with saucepans and rolling-pins.

At a signal from Badsleeves, a hundred bolts of heavy magic smashed against the iron shutters and reduced them to dust. With blood-curdling shrieks, the flying witches swooped.

Mrs Abercrombie was a clever old witch and horribly strong, but without the special protection of the Power Hat she was no match for the fifty hand-picked witches of the flying squad. Twenty of them held her down, while the humans tied her arms and legs with a thick rope. She wriggled furiously, like a gigantic, angry slug.

Mrs Wilkins was caught trying to sneak away up the chimney. She was arrested and tied up next to Mrs Abercrombie.

"You said there wouldn't be any danger!" she shouted. "That's the last time I vote for YOU!"

"Where are the children?" clamoured the villagers. "Give us our children – you FIEND!"

Mendax jumped on his hind legs and grabbed the bars of his cage with his front paws.

"Noshie! Skirty! In the cellar!"

Old Noshie and Skirty Marm were having the time of their lives. Skirty had always dreamed of flying with the Number One Broom Squadron, known on Witch Island as the "Death-or-Glory Brooms". With whoops of triumph, they wrenched open the cellar door and hurtled down the hundreds of steps to the secret cave.

Poor Amy Noggs screamed to see more witchy figures looming through the shadows. But Emma Blenkinsop recognized her two friends from the Brownies at once.

"We're safe!" she cried, giving each witch a hug. "We knew you'd come for us!"

"Mrs A. can't beat US!" boasted Skirty Marm. "Not while I'm wearing the Power Hat!"

"What's so special about that old thing?" asked Ben Blenkinsop. "It looks like a tea cosy."

"You'll find out," chuckled Old Noshie. "Come on, let's get you out of here."

The two witches led the children up the stone steps to the cottage kitchen. There were cries of joy as they ran into the arms of their parents.

"Thank you! Thank you!" Mr Babbercorn shook Badsleeves's hand so hard that her hat fell off. "You're our heroines!"

"I don't normally hold with magic," said Mr Noggs, "but you've been very helpful."

"Hear hear!" said all the other humans.

"YEUCH!" complained Mrs Abercrombie. "Disgusting human MUSH – no self-respecting witch would have stood it in my day!"

But Badsleeves and her flying squad looked rather pleased. Nobody had ever thanked them before or called them heroines. It was certainly a very unusual way to spend Hallowe'en.

"What shall we do with Mrs A.?" asked Old Noshie.

"We could kill her," suggested Badsleeves. "It

seems a pity not to have that State Funeral – I've already written my speech."

"You won't kill me!" raged Mrs Abercrombie. "Because I've got one more thing you want!"

She pursed up her rubbery lips until they looked like the nozzle of a vacuum-cleaner. Then she sucked hard. The door of Mendax's cage flew open. The little cat clung on with all his might, but it was useless. He was sucked right across the room and Mrs Abercrombie, with a loud gulp, swallowed him whole.

"You nasty, evil, beastly, wicked—" gasped the vicar, turning deathly pale.

"You could always have him back," said Mrs Abercrombie, "if you swap him for the HAT!"

"No way!" said Badsleeves firmly.

"Please!" begged poor Mr Snelling. "Mendax ran away to protect the witches because he knew he was powerless once Mrs Abercrombie got his code! Please don't desert him now!"

The witches tried everything.

Watched by the sniffing vicar, the fifty witches and the terrified villagers, they tried finding spells, rescue spells, shrinking spells (for Mendax) and stun spells (for Mrs Abercrombie). Old Noshie even tried jumping up and down on Mrs Abercrombie's stomach. Nothing worked.

Sorry, typed the Power Hat. *He's inside her, and even my magic cannot touch him.*

"Oh, Mendax!" cried the vicar. "Are you in pain? Can you hear me?"

"Let's be thankful for small mercies," said the muffled voice of Mendax from inside the ex-queen's stomach. "At least she didn't chew me."

"Give me my Hat," said Mrs Abercrombie, "and I'll let him go."

"Don't you dare!" shouted Badsleeves. "Human children are one matter, but I'm not losing my government for the sake of a CAT!"

"The Chancellor is right," Mendax's voice said bravely. "What is one small cat against the freedom of Witch Island? You'd better leave me here, to be DIGESTED."

"We appreciate this, Cat," said Badsleeves. "I shall order a statue to be built for you."

"Something simple in black marble, perhaps," said Mendax. "Yes, that would be very nice. It's a slow, horrible death, but I am happy to lay down my poor life for the sake of the Greater Good."

"You always were a noble cat," said poor Mr Snelling. "I'm going to miss you so much, I think my heart will break!"

"Think of me sometimes," said Mendax. "Put a little stone in some shady nook. And on it write these simple words –

Stranger! Pause and shed a Tear for
MENDAX
("Colonel Mendy" of Fungus Gulch)
Revoltingly DIGESTED
For the Cause of LIBERTY!"

102

"Oh, that's beautiful!" said Mr Snelling, busily writing it down in his notebook.

All the villagers, and even several of the hand-picked witches, sniffed.

"Typical Mendax!" murmured Mr Babbercorn to Alice, wiping his eyes. "I'd swear he's enjoying this!"

Mrs Abercrombie laughed nastily. "You won't be able to stand his screams of agony for long! You'll soon be BEGGING me to take the Hat!"

"Fiddlesticks!" grunted an ancient dusty voice. "You always were a power-mad witch, Euphemia Abercrombie – and it's time you were taught a lesson."

The dusty cobwebby figure of Mouldypage shuffled through the crowd.

For the very first time, Mrs Abercrombie looked alarmed. She had been at school with Mouldypage, and no living witch knew her better.

"You think you're so clever," said Mouldypage. "You think you know everything about the Power Hat."

"I know more than you do!" blustered Mrs Abercrombie. "I won the Golden Broom at school!"

"Only because you CHEATED," said Mouldypage with a dry chuckle. "Some things never change! I didn't much care at the time, because I was only interested in books. But Witch Island is much more comfortable now you've gone. So I think I should remind you who's REALLY the smartest witch of all!"

She turned to Skirty Marm.

"Ignorant Red-Stocking," she croaked. "This is an emergency. You must ask the Power Hat for a page of the FORBIDDEN BOOK."

"NO!" bellowed Mrs Abercrombie. She began to thrash about madly in her ropes. "You're bluffing – the Forbidden Book doesn't exist!"

Trembling with excitement, Skirty Marm shut her eyes. The green letters were already inside her head.

Yes! At last – someone who knows how to use me properly! the Power Hat had typed. *Now, pay attention . . .*

A breathless silence fell over the cottage. Witches and humans watched as Skirty Marm read the Hat's instructions.

When Skirty Marm opened her eyes, she was very pale.

"Untie Mrs Abercrombie!"

All the witches began to babble and shriek with fury.

"You're CRAZY!" shouted Badsleeves. "She'll kill us all!"

"Noshie," said Skirty Marm, "untie her!"

Old Noshie did not like it any more than the others – but she trusted Skirty Marm. Shaking like a pale green jelly, she undid the ex-queen's ropes.

"Mrs Abercrombie," said Skirty Marm solemnly, "hand over Mendax – and you can have the Hat!"

"Leave me here!" Mendax cried, from inside the Royal stomach. "I'm only a little lying cat! What am I worth when weighed against the lives of all these witches?"

A deathly hush suddenly fell over all the witches.

"I've shut them up with a temporary silence spell," said Mouldypage. "I can't stand noise. Now, get on with it, Red-Stocking!"

Mrs Abercrombie was breathing hard, as if she had been running. "Come to me, beloved Power Hat!" she panted. "Together, we will reign in WICKEDNESS!"

Skirty Marm slowly took the Power Hat off her head and held it out to Mrs Abercrombie.

Five of the silenced witches fainted.

Her face alight with terrible joy, Mrs Abercrombie gave a mighty burp and Mendax shot out of her mouth. With a "miaow" of shock, he landed in the arms of the vicar.

Mrs Abercrombie's hairy fist closed around the Power Hat. And then an extraordinary thing happened.

The bobble of the Hat burst into a ball of scarlet flame. The flames consumed the rest of the Hat, and Mrs Abercrombie dropped it with a yelp of pain. The blazing Power Hat slowly rose into the air. For a moment, it burned so brightly that everyone had to shade their eyes. Then it crumbled away into black cinders – and disappeared.

On the empty air, a thread of black smoke briefly formed the word

"GOODBYE".

The amazed silence stretched on and on, even when Mouldypage removed her spell.

"Gone!" whispered Chancellor Badsleeves in amazement. "The greatest treasure of our Island

– and our greatest CURSE! Gone!"

"The Power Hat didn't mean to be a curse," Skirty Marm said loyally. "It only did bad things because Mrs A. made it!"

"And since it lived with these humans," added Old Noshie, "it wanted to be good."

"How disgusting!" muttered Mouldypage. "Dratted humans and their SOPPY ways!"

"You don't approve of us, yet you've been very kind to us!" Mr Snelling said. He was stroking Mendax and smiling all over his round face. "We're so grateful!"

"Oh, I didn't do it for you," croaked Mouldypage. "I wanted to get my own back on Euphemia Abercrombie. I would have won that Golden Broom if she hadn't nicked my best spell. Well, we're even now, Euphemia – that'll teach you to snoop in other people's pencil cases!"

Mrs Abercrombie had not made one sound since the vanishing of the Power Hat. Her hideous face had turned an unhealthy yellow.

"Gone!" she choked. "My life's work – ruined! Old Noshie and Skirty Marm, you'll PAY for this!"

"Take no notice," said Mouldypage. "She'll need all her magic when I've finished with her!"

She gabbled a spell in witch-Latin. There was just enough time to see Mrs Abercrombie's expression of terror before the two ancient witches vanished into thin air.

Witches and humans were left in the cottage kitchen, staring at the space where the evil ex-queen had been.

Mr Babbercorn was the first to recover. He hugged Old Noshie and Skirty Marm.

"Please forgive me for not listening to your warning," he said. "There's a lot I still don't understand about all this – for instance, how did you know Mrs Brightpie had Mendax? How did he get the message to you?"

"We might as well tell the truth now," said Old Noshie.

"You're rubbish at keeping secrets!" grumbled Skirty Marm.

"I'm afraid we cast a small spell on Thomas," Noshie said.

"A spell!" gasped Alice.

"Well, it was actually quite a big spell. To make him understand animals. That's how he got the message."

"It's his christening present," confessed Skirty Marm. "We just couldn't bear to give him something ordinary. Please don't be cross!"

Alice hugged Thomas – she was carrying him in a sling around her neck. To the surprise of the two guilty witches, she and Mr Babbercorn started laughing.

"I should be cross," said Alice. "But I don't mind him keeping this present as long as you promise not to cast any more spells on him!"

"Hurrah!" cried Thomas – a piece of Babyspeak that everyone understood.

"We promise!" chorused the witches.

Mr Noggs had been whispering with the other humans. He stepped forward, clearing his throat importantly.

"Ladies and – er – witches," he said. "We realize that you have missed your usual Hallowe'en Ball, through helping us. As a mark of our gratitude, we'd like to give you a *party*."

And this is how the most unusual Hallowe'en party in the world was held, in the vicarage garden of Tranters End.

Mr Snelling telephoned the jazz band that sometimes played in the local pub. Alice made another tub of Instant Whip. Everyone in the village cleared larders and fridges to give Badsleeves and her witches the greatest feast of their lives. Old Noshie and Skirty Marm threw themselves into mad witch-dances round the blazing bonfires. They taught Mr Babbercorn the Donkey-Dive, the Ear-Grabber and other traditional dances. He enjoyed it very much and only stopped when someone shouted, "Take your partners for the SLOW BUM-KICK!"

"This is the best Hallowe'en Ball since you two sang your song!" declared Chancellor Badsleeves. "I'm going to have trouble scaring this lot next year!"

Old Noshie and Skirty Marm grinned.

"Oh, humans are all right," said Skirty Marm.

"When you get to know them," added Old Noshie.

Witch You Were Here

For Leonora and William

1

Away From It All

In the vicarage garden, in a quiet village called Tranters End, two witches were rainbathing. This is what witches do instead of sunbathing. Like frogs and snakes and other leathery-skinned creatures, they don't like too much sun.

One of the witches – Old Noshie – smiled as she felt the cool raindrops pattering on her head. "Cor, this is lovely!" she said. "We've had such nasty hot weather lately." She popped a passing spider into her mouth.

Skirty Marm lay back comfortably in her deck chair. "I've never understood what the humans see in that sun," she declared. "Nasty, vulgar, flaming thing – thank goodness for rain! Ah, this makes me think of old times!"

Both witches sighed, remembering the beautiful damp chilliness of their old home. Old Noshie and Skirty Marm had grown up on

Witch Island, which is a bleak and rocky place. The weather is usually wet, and the sun is always hidden behind a thick grey duvet of cloud. Nowadays, they lived happily in the church belfry at Tranters End, and dearly loved the humans of the village – but they still missed the Witch Island weather.

Mrs Abercrombie, the wicked Queen of Witch Island, had banished Old Noshie and Skirty Marm for one hundred years, because they had committed a dreadful crime. They had sung a rude song about Mrs Abercrombie at the Hallowe'en Ball (see *The Bumper Book of Famous Rude Songs*, Belch & Squelch, 9w. shillings). The two homeless witches had found shelter in Tranters End, and the local people were now quite used to occasional bursts of magic.

"Where is everyone?" wondered Skirty Marm. "It's a shame to be stuck indoors on a gorgeous day like this!"

"Mr B. and Alice have taken Thomas into town," said Old Noshie, picking spider-legs out of her teeth. "Mr Snelling's in the study – and goodness knows where Mendax has got to. I haven't seen him for days."

Mr Babbercorn was the young curate of St Tranters Church. He lived at the vicarage, with his wife Alice and their baby son, Thomas. The Babbercorns were the witches' best human friends. They had been bridesmaids at the wedding of Mr B. and Alice, and they were little Thomas's godmothers. Old Noshie and Skirty Marm were also extremely fond of the vicar, Mr Snelling – a very kind, very plump and rather greedy man.

Mendax was the vicar's adopted cat. He had once been a cat-slave on Witch Island, and he could talk (which was upsetting for strangers). In fact, Mendax talked all the time. He did the shopping, cooking and cleaning, and bossed the vicar from morning till night.

Skirty Marm snorted scornfully – she never could forget that Mendax had once been a spy, working for Mrs Abercrombie.

"That cat is up to something!" she declared. "He's been acting very strangely ever since he went back to Witch Island for that weekend break."

"He keeps sneaking off to the shed," Old Noshie agreed. "He's put black paper over the window so nobody can peek inside."

"He needn't be so SNOOTY!" sniffed Skirty Marm. "Whatever he's up to, I wish he'd let us join in! It's been so boring here since the Power Hat left."

Old Noshie shuddered. "I'm glad it's gone. If this is boring, it suits me fine."

The Power Hat had caused a lot of trouble for the witches in the past, and put them in terrible danger. It was a witch's hat, two metres tall, with an everlasting candle burning at its point. No living witch knew all its secrets, but its magic was immense. The witch who wore the Power Hat was the strongest witch in all the world and, until Old Noshie and Skirty Marm returned to Witch Island after their banishment and stole the Hat, it had belonged to Mrs Abercrombie.

Without it, she was nothing more than an extremely clever but ordinary old witch. For the first time, the witches of the Island had a proper election and threw out their evil queen.

Since then, Mrs Abercrombie had spent all her huge fortune trying to snatch the Power Hat back, but Old Noshie and Skirty Marm had always managed to keep it out of her evil hands. You will not be surprised to hear that Mrs Abercrombie now hated the two witches. She swore that she would kill them the minute the Hat was back on her head and her gigantic bottom was back on the throne.

Then, last Hallowe'en, the Power Hat had burst into flames and VANISHED.

Nobody knew what had happened to Mrs Abercrombie. She had not been seen since, by witch or human – but she often appeared in the nightmares of Old Noshie and Skirty Marm. She was hugely fat, and her terrible wickedness made her ugly face even more hideous. Her chin was covered by a straggly grey beard (usually full of half-digested insects), her teeth were made of metal and her eyes were little and curranty, and incredibly mean.

It made Old Noshie shiver just to think of her. "When Mrs A. was chasing that dratted Power Hat," she said, "I never had a minute of peace. I was always scared she'd suddenly pounce on me!"

Old Noshie was a plump, easy-going witch, with a bald head, which she usually covered with a blue wig, and a skin of startling bright green (she glowed in the dark, and the vicar often used her to find things in the cellar). She was not particularly clever, and not at all brave.

But Skirty Marm was always getting mixed up in dangerous adventures – and Old Noshie had never done anything without Skirty Marm. She had followed her faithfully, since the pair were little witches at school.

Skirty Marm was a long, skinny witch, with fizzing red eyes and a clump of purple hair. At school, she had won every prize going – including the Spitting Shield, the Golden Broom and (for thirty-six years in a row) the Spellbinder's Medal. It was hard for a talented witch like Skirty to give up magic, but Mr Babbercorn did not approve, and she had promised to cast no more spells without his permission.

Mostly, she kept her promise pretty well. Instead of brewing potions, Skirty Marm spent her time working for Brownie badges and learning songs at the Old Folks' Drop-In Club. She and Old Noshie were allowed to belong to both the Brownies and the Old Folks' Club because of their strange mixture of ages. Although they were both over one hundred and fifty years old, which is ancient for a human, they were only young Red-Stocking witches.

If you want to know the age of a witch, take

a good look at the colour of her stockings. Here is a simple guide:

1. YELLOW-STOCKINGS – baby witches, under 100 years old, still at school.
2. RED-STOCKINGS – witches over the age of 100 years.
3. GREEN-STOCKINGS – witches over the age of 200 years.
4. PURPLE-STOCKINGS – witches over the age of 300 years.

Generally speaking, if you come across a witch in purple stockings, you should take extra care. Some of the senior witches on Witch Island were many hundreds of years old (Mrs Abercrombie was nearly a thousand), and they came from the days of the old fairy tales, when witches really were very wicked. Like many elderly people, they did not take kindly to changes. Many of the Purple-Stockings, and some of the Greens, hated the newly elected Red-Stocking government of Witch Island. They missed the good old days, when they had been allowed to keep cat-slaves and bully the younger generations.

Skirty Marm did not miss those grim times,

but she was finding her non-magical life with the humans far too quiet.

"Nosh, do you know what I'd like now?" she blurted out suddenly. "An ADVENTURE!"

"I wouldn't," said Old Noshie. "Adventures are scary."

Before Skirty Marm could argue, a woman's voice called, "Witches! Biscuits!"

Alice, a smiling young woman with curly brown hair, stood at the back door of the vicarage. Mrs Abercrombie had once turned Alice into a snail, and the witches had saved her.

She had grown very fond of them and often bought them treats.

The two witches loved human biscuits. They leapt up at once and rushed into the kitchen, making wet tracks all over the floor.

"Sorry," said Old Noshie. "We've been RAINBATHING."

"Never mind," said Alice. "Have a Jammy Dodger – I know they're your favourites."

"Hello witches!" shouted Thomas, in his high chair. He was nearly a year old, and he could say two words in English ("cat" and "Daddy"). But he spoke another language – a series of burbles and squawks known as Babyspeak, which both the witches knew.

"Quick, Noshie!" Thomas cried, in Babyspeak. "Get me a biscuit while she's not looking! She won't let me have another, because I keep throwing them on the floor!"

"Don't give Thomas a biscuit," Alice said, without turning round. "He'll only throw it on the floor."

Alice did not know Babyspeak, and did not need to.

Mr Babbercorn was making tea for himself and Alice, two cups of muddy pond water for the witches, and a beaker of juice for Thomas. He was a pale, weedy young man. Today, his thin face was anxious. Both he and his wife seemed rather nervous.

When they were all sitting round the table, he cleared his throat.

"Witches, there's something we want to tell you," he announced. "Alice and I – well, we've decided to take Thomas away for a summer holiday. It'll be our first holiday as a real family. We're off to Gusty Bay, where we went for our honeymoon." He faltered, and his pale face turned red. "The thing is, witches, we – er – we won't be taking anyone with us."

There was a long silence. Both Mr Babbercorn and Alice looked uncomfortable.

Old Noshie said, "Good idea – we don't need anyone else."

Skirty Marm's red eyes were fizzing dangerously. "You silly old PLOP," she growled. "He means he DOESN'T WANT US!"

"*What*?" Old Noshie could not believe her green ears.

"Please don't be offended!" begged Alice. "Two weeks on our own – it's not much to ask!"

"I've been looking jolly pale lately," said Old

Noshie in a very offended voice. "Two weeks by the sea would put the cabbages back in my cheeks."

"Don't expect kindness from these SELFISH humans!" stormed Skirty Marm. "All they care about is having a good time without us. We'll be stuck here, in horrible blazing sunshine, and they'll be living it up on a rainy beach!"

Old Noshie's lips began to wobble. "It's not fair, and you're being very MEAN. We wouldn't be any trouble!"

"I'm afraid not," Mr Babbercorn said, gently but firmly. "The Sea Breeze Guest House doesn't take witches."

Skirty Marm scowled. "You should have booked one that said 'witches welcome'."

"It doesn't mean we don't love you," Alice said. "All we want is a little time on our own. Away from it all."

Skirty Marm leapt up, tossing her purple hair proudly. "Come, Noshie. Let us not dirty our rags in this SMELLY place. We know when we're NOT WANTED."

Skirty Marm stomped out of the house, followed by Old Noshie, who was crying noisily. Her wails could be heard all the way up the one hundred and eighty-six belfry steps.

"Are we being selfish?" Alice asked her husband fearfully. "I feel awful!"

Mr Babbercorn squeezed her hand. "Don't worry. They'll soon get over it."

The witches were scandalized and outraged. How could Mr Babbercorn and Alice dream of taking a holiday without them? The sheer selfishness of it amazed them. They were sure everyone in the village would agree and feel very sorry for them – but nobody seemed to think the Babbercorns were being at all unreasonable.

"It does everyone good to get away sometimes," said Mrs Tucker at the Post Office, who was also Brown Owl. "I'm off to Spain next week."

Even Mr Snelling, who had not been invited to Gusty Bay either, refused to take the witches' side.

"A change is as good as a rest," he said. "I'm going on holiday myself, you know."

"But you never go away!" cried Skirty Marm.

Mr Snelling smiled. "I'm going to stay in a castle in France and have very posh cookery lessons."

"Ha!" snapped Skirty Marm rudely. "Mendax will never allow it!"

"As a matter of fact," said the vicar, "it was his idea."

"What? Eh?" Skirty Marm was instantly suspicious. Mendax hated letting the vicar out of his sight, in case he took up with another cat.

"That little cat is so considerate!" Mr Snelling went on happily. "He says it'll do me good to get away from it all, at the same time as the others. He says he'll hold the fort here – he's even arranged for Father Baggins from St Martin's to take the services!" He giggled suddenly. "It'll certainly do me good to get away from Mendax's nagging. Oh, I can't wait – two whole weeks of making fancy pastry, with nobody mewing at me to trim my nose-hairs!"

"Well, don't expect us to hang around here, with nobody but that sneaky little bag of fur!" snapped Skirty Marm. "Noshie and me are having a holiday too. So there!"

Old Noshie gaped – this was the first she had heard of it. But she had the sense not to annoy Skirty Marm by asking questions. She didn't say a word until they were safely back in their belfry.

"How can we go on holiday, Skirt? We haven't got any human money, and holidays cost ever such a lot!"

"Pooh, we don't need *money*!" Skirty Marm said grandly. "We're witches, aren't we?"

"Yes," Old Noshie said, starting to look worried, "but we promised Mr B. we wouldn't do any magic without asking him!"

"Pish and posh!" snarled Skirty Marm. "Why should we keep any promises to that mean curate?"

"He doesn't deserve it," Old Noshie agreed, with a sniff. "But where are we going for our holiday?"

"Gusty Bay, of course!" said Skirty Marm. "That Mr Babbercorn might think he's getting away from it all, but he's not getting away from US!"

2

What Mendax Was Up To

It was a wonderful idea, and Old Noshie and Skirty Marm were very pleased with themselves. Every time Mr Babbercorn or Alice mentioned Gusty Bay, the two witches burst into giggles and pinched each other with secret glee. Deep down, they knew that following the humans on their holiday was not a very kind thing to do, but they were both too angry about being left out to care.

"Mr B. doesn't OWN Gusty Bay!" Skirty Marm declared. "He can't stop us having our holiday there too!"

"No," Old Noshie said, a little doubtfully. "But, Skirty, we don't know anything about human holidays. What sort of luggage will we need?"

Skirty Marm hated admitting she did not know something. "Oh – I expect it'll be just like

Slime Regis."

"Really?" Old Noshie brightened. Slime Regis was the only holiday resort on Witch Island. It was a grim huddle of black cliffs, lashed by rain and buffeted by freezing gales. Skirty Marm had once won a holiday for two there in a burping contest, and they had both loved it. Old Noshie decided that if Gusty Bay was anything like Slime Regis, things were looking up. "What a pity we couldn't bring our swimming-sacks when we were banished."

"Humans take buckets and spades on their holidays," Skirty Marm said knowledgeably.

Old Noshie was puzzled. "Why?"

"I-I don't know," Skirty Marm admitted, with a frown. "We'd better ask Alice. But we'll have to make sure she doesn't find out where we're going. Leave most of the talking to me."

"Righto," said Old Noshie. "I know I'm rubbish at keeping secrets."

Alice was glad the witches had stopped being cross with her – but she was rather puzzled by their behaviour. For one thing, they kept bursting into giggles for no reason that she could see. And they began bombarding her with all kinds of odd questions about the seaside. Alice still felt bad about leaving the witches behind, and she answered them patiently.

"The buckets and spades are for building sandcastles on the beach," she explained.

"A strange custom," remarked Skirty Marm.

"I wish you'd tell us where you're going," Alice said. "It's obviously somewhere beside the sea."

She could not understand why this made the two witches giggle again.

"Yes, it is!" shouted Old Noshie.

Skirty Marm gave her friend a quick biff, to remind her not to tell.

"I'm afraid we can't say where we're going, Alice," she said firmly. "You'd only get JEALOUS."

Mr Babbercorn would have suspected something by now, but Alice was not a suspicious woman.

"Well, I only know about Gusty Bay," she said innocently, "but most seaside places have the same things. I'd be happy to give you advice."

"We'd like to know," Old Noshie said, "what humans wear in the sea."

"Gracious," said Alice, "haven't you ever

seen a swimming costume? Here." She bent down to pull something out of the washing machine. "This is the swimming costume I was wearing when I first met Cuthbert."

Old Noshie and Skirty Marm were staring, with gaping mouths and eyes, at the tiny piece of striped material Alice was holding.

"Where's the rest of it?" asked Old Noshie.

"This is all of it," Alice said.

"What – THAT?" shrieked Skirty Marm. The two witches burst into howls of laughter. They laughed so much that Alice became a little embarrassed.

"You can't wear that teeny thing!" gasped Old Noshie. "Everybody will see the shape of your – *ha ha ha* – the shape of your – *hee hee hee* – your BOTTOM!"

The word "bottom" made the witches laugh until they had to lie down on the kitchen table.

When they had recovered, Alice asked curiously, "What do witches wear when they go swimming?"

"A SWIMMING-SACK, of course!" cried Skirty Marm, wiping her eyes. "It's a huge piece of material, with holes for your face and hands and feet."

"You leave your pointed hat in the changing-cave," added Old Noshie. "And your stockings."

"But NOT your bloomers," Skirty Marm said. "Or someone's sure to NICK them."

Alice struggled not to laugh, knowing this would annoy the witches. "Humans find it difficult to swim if they're weighed down by too much material," she said. "And we don't think it's rude to show the SHAPE of your bottom – just your ACTUAL bottom."

This time, realizing she was serious, the witches did not laugh.

Old Noshie's green face was shocked. "Well, don't expect me to go in the sea in one of those teeny stripy things!"

"Certainly NOT," Skirty Marm said firmly. "Humans have no DIGNITY."

Alice could not help laughing now. She tried to turn it into a cough. "Is there anything else I can tell you?"

"What's the food like?" asked greedy Old Noshie.

"Lovely," said Alice. "That's why you take extra spending-money to the seaside – to buy candy-floss and crab sandwiches and ice creams and chips and sticks of rock—"

"Wow!" murmured Old Noshie, licking her green lips.

Skirty Marm was less interested in eating. "What sort of things do you DO at the seaside?"

"Well," Alice said thoughtfully, "when the weather's nice, you sit on the beach, and play in the sea. And when it isn't very nice, you go to the boating-pool, or the amusement arcade on the pier. That's the other reason you need spending-money. For instance, just a short game of Crazy Golf costs fifty pence."

"That sounds good!" Skirty Marm was fascinated. "What is Crazy Golf?"

"It's a bit like ordinary golf," Alice said, "because you have to knock balls into little holes. But in Crazy Golf, the holes are very funny and surprising."

Old Noshie blurted out, "Is the rainbathing good at Gusty Bay?"

Skirty Marm hissed, "Shut up!" and pinched Old Noshie's nose.

"The rainbathing's very good there, I should think," Alice said. She did not seem to have noticed the pinch. "Sometimes it rains so hard that there's nowhere to go except the slide-show at the Town Hall."

"Cor," whispered Old Noshie, "doesn't it sound BRILL?"

"Not half!" said Skirty Marm. And then she remembered what Alice had said about spending-money. Her grey face became gloomy. "But doesn't it sound EXPENSIVE? Excuse us, Alice – we have to look in our piggy bank."

The witches' piggy bank was not a pig, but a little china cottage. This was where they kept their human money. Mr Babbercorn gave them fifty pence a week each. They earned a bit more by doing odd jobs around the village, such as flying up on their broomsticks to clear people's gutters.

Back in the belfry, Old Noshie and Skirty Marm opened the cottage and emptied their savings out on the dusty floor. Skirty Marm counted the coins. When she had finished, she looked gloomier than ever.

"Three pounds and seventy-two pence. That's not going to get us very far. Noshie, we have to find ourselves some more money."

Old Noshie was worried. "But where? Mr B. and the vicar need all their money for their own holidays. We don't know anyone else we can ask – except Mendax."

Skirty Marm's red eyes flashed. "Mendax! Of course!"

It was well-known to the witches that Mendax had a nice bundle of human money hidden away. Mr Snelling had given it to him. Where his cat was concerned, the vicar's head was as soft as his heart.

"Huh! We won't get anything out of Mendax!" Old Noshie said crossly. "You know how mean he is."

Skirty Marm was grinning and red sparks were fizzing in her eyes. Her great mind had begun to plot and plan.

"Oh yes!" she cackled. "But I also know Mendax is up to no good. If we can just find out what it is – we've GOT him!"

Mendax certainly had been behaving very strangely over the past few weeks. The little cat had started disappearing for hours on end. He would come home very late, often covered in odd substances – mud, oil, seaweed, even beetroot soup once – and he never offered a word of explanation. Most unusually for this neat and elegant animal, he had started to be careless about the housework. He forgot the shopping. He mixed up the whites and the coloureds in the washing, and he kept burning dinners.

Mr Snelling and the Babbercorns were too busy preparing for their holidays to take much notice, but the witches were watching Mendax very closely. One evening, they saw him limp into the vicarage kitchen with his back-left paw in a bandage. They were shocked to hear him telling the vicar he had been in a fight with the cat from the Post Office.

"What a WHOPPER!" Skirty Marm said to Old Noshie later. "The Post Office cat is ill with a bad ear – he hasn't even been out for days. This means Mendax is back to his old ways!"

In Latin, "Mendax" means "liar", and it was a very suitable name for this particular cat. He loved to tell stories as tall as skyscrapers.

Now that the witches knew Mendax was hiding something, they watched him like a pair of hawks. Every day, they took it in turns to crouch beside the belfry window, watching the garden shed through a plastic telescope Old Noshie had got for Christmas. But they saw nothing interesting. Mendax stayed at home, resting his hurt paw. He sat on the lawn reading a book, which was very boring to spy on. The witches began to worry that they would never catch him out.

"And then we'll never have enough human money for our secret trip to Gusty Bay!" Skirty Marm said impatiently on the day before the Babbercorns and Mr Snelling went on holiday. "But he must do something soon – that cat is the reason everyone's going away! He made them think of it! He wants them out of the way! Mr B. and the vicar don't realize it, but they're playing right into his crafty little paws!"

Today it was Old Noshie's turn to watch through the telescope.

"Look out – here he comes!" she shouted suddenly.

At last, far below, they saw the little black cat creeping out of the back door of the vicarage, looking extremely shifty and furtive. He was walking on his hind legs, and carrying a plastic bag in his front paws. After a nervous glance around, he darted across the lawn and shut himself in the shed.

"Action stations!" cried Skirty Marm.

The two witches jumped on their broomsticks and zoomed down to the garden. Old Noshie started giggling again.

Skirty Marm nudged her sternly. "Shut up! And stand back while I break this lock."

Mendax had put a stout padlock on the shed door, and he kept the key fastened to his collar. This kept the humans away, but it was no protection against witches. Skirty Marm muttered a simple lock-busting spell, and the padlock flew open.

"AHA!" roared the witches. "CAUGHT YOU!"

They leapt into the shed – then stopped short, and gaped around in amazement.

There was no sign of Mendax. The shed was crammed with deck chairs, garden tools, crusty tins of paint, and the rowing machine the vicar had once bought to make himself slimmer. All this was pushed against the walls. A large space had been cleared in the middle of the floor.

Old Noshie and Skirty Marm rubbed their eyes in disbelief.

"Where did he go?" gasped Old Noshie.

They had seen Mendax creeping in, but now the only clue that he had ever been here was his plastic carrier bag, lying on a pile of flowerpots.

Skirty Marm snatched it, to look inside. "Sandwiches," she said in disgust. "Fish-paste sandwiches! What's going on?"

As if in answer to that question, there was a sudden, blinding flash of white light.

"AARRGH!" shrieked the witches.

The empty space on the floor was now filled with a crazy machine, which looked like a cross between a sledge, a car engine and a dentist's chair. Mendax was perched at the front of this contraption. On his small head he wore a metal helmet covered with springs. He was very startled – and very annoyed – to see the witches.

"Drat," he mewed sourly. "What are you two doing here? Can't a cat have any privacy?"

But the witches were not listening. They had recognized the strange machine at once, though they only knew it from school books and pictures in the Witch Island newspaper. It was so astonishing that they stared at it in silence, for nearly ten minutes.

"Well, well, well!" Skirty Marm said at last. A wicked grin broke out on her grey face. "So *this* is why you keep disappearing! *This* is why

you're so full of secrets! You've got your paws on a TIME MACHINE!"

Old Noshie prodded the Time Machine with her finger. Mendax immediately whipped a little cloth out of his collar and wiped it. "Don't make smears!"

"Sorry," said Old Noshie. "But I've never seen one of these in real life. Where did you get it?"

Mendax was still fiddling with his cloth. He did not seem to have heard.

"OI!" shouted Skirty Marm. "My friend asked you a question! Where did you get this thing?"

"Oh, I picked it up when I had that weekend in Witch Island," Mendax said casually. "It's the new economy model. It comes in a flat-pack, with simple instructions for fitting together."

Skirty Marm laughed unkindly. "Cor, there's an AWFUL smell of LIES in here!"

Like many terrible liars, Mendax was always furious when anyone accused him of lying.

"It's perfectly TRUE!" he snapped. "Look at the box if you don't believe me!"

"You NICKED it," said Skirty Marm, grinning gleefully.

"How *dare* you?" spat Mendax.

"Oh, come off it," Skirty said scornfully. "You know the laws about Time Machines on Witch Island. You need to be a Purple-Stocking, with a special licence signed by the Chancellor. You'd never be allowed to buy one in a million years – so you STOLE one!"

Mendax's bright green eyes flickered from one witch to another. When he spoke again, his voice was very small and sulky.

"All right. I stole it. But I was desperate. I BEG you not to give me away to the Witch Police!"

"We'll have to see about that," Skirty Marm said gleefully. For once, she had Mendax exactly where she wanted him. Stealing a Time Machine was a serious offence on Witch Island. If the Witch Police found out what he had done, no human help could save Mendax from being arrested and sent to prison for ages.

"Where have you been in it?" Old Noshie asked curiously.

"Oh – here and there," said Mendax.

Skirty Marm let out a loud, mocking cackle. "Nosh, I've guessed! I know why he wanted it! Hee hee hee! He's been at the BATTLE OF

FUNGUS GULCH!"

Fungus Gulch was a famous battle in Witch history. It had happened many years before Mendax was born – but this had never stopped him telling stories about how he had been there. At last he had found a way of turning his boastful fantasies into truth.

He scowled. "I suppose you might as well know the whole story. Yes, you're right – Fungus Gulch is the reason I've been away so much."

Old Noshie chortled. "Now you'll have to find something new to lie about!"

Mendax ignored this. "I'm working on something very important. I have to keep going back to the same place in the Battle – because I want to be in the history books. I want to be a FAMOUS HISTORICAL CHARACTER."

"So what are you going to do at Fungus Gulch to get yourself mentioned in the history books?" Skirty Marm asked jeeringly. "A tap-dance?"

"I'll admit," Mendax said, in his most dignified mew, "I've set my sights rather high. I want to lead the Charge of the Pointed Brooms."

This made both witches howl with laughter. The Charge of the Pointed Brooms was one of

145

the most famous incidents in Witch history – rather like the Charge of the Light Brigade in our world. The idea of a small black cat leading the attack was hilarious.

"It's going to take me some time," Mendax said stiffly. "I have to go back again and again, changing the history bit by bit – I'm still trying to get near the front."

"And you wanted the humans out of the way," said Skirty Marm, "because you knew Mr B. and the vicar would be HOPPING MAD if they discovered you tinkering about with such serious magic!"

Mendax's black fur bristled. "Yes, I'm afraid Mr Snelling has some rather old-fashioned notions about magic. I sent him on holiday to stop him asking awkward questions. Now, if you'll excuse me, I must return to the Charge. I only popped back because I forgot my sandwiches."

"Not so fast!" said Skirty Marm. "What's to stop me and Noshie calling the Witch Police and telling the vicar?"

"Oh, I SEE," Mendax mewed icily. "And what do you want for keeping quiet?"

"We'll take the sandwiches, for a start!" said

Old Noshie, with her mouth full of fish-paste.

"And we need to borrow your SAVINGS!" said Skirty Marm craftily.

First, Mendax looked furious. Then he tried to look casual. "My savings? Yes, I do have one or two little coins in my meagre hoard – perhaps twenty pence—"

"Even I know that's a LIE," Old Noshie interrupted cheerfully. "You're the richest cat in the whole village, because you made Mr Snelling PAY you for writing his sermons!"

"You've got a sock stuffed with money!" said Skirty Marm. "You keep it hidden in your cat-duvet!"

"Oh, you've LOOKED, have you?" Mendax snarled.

Skirty Marm put her face close to his. "You have to lend us your money, so we can buy nice things on our holiday."

"We'll pay you back," added Old Noshie. "One day."

Mendax flicked out his claws angrily. "You can go to prison for blackmail, you know!"

"Good, we can all be in prison together," said Skirty Marm.

There was a long, long silence. Then Mendax

sighed, and smoothed his whiskers. "Oh, all right. You can borrow my money. You know where it is."

"Hurrah!" yelled Skirty Marm. "Thanks, Mendax! Have a nice time at Fungus Gulch!" She danced out of the garden shed, beaming like a lighthouse.

Old Noshie had to trot to keep up. She was not beaming, and her breathless voice was worried. "Skirt, if Mr B. finds out we did this, he'll be ever so cross! Crosser than he's EVER been!"

This had already occurred to Skirty Marm, but she was doing her best not to think about it.

"I don't care!" she shouted. "So what if we've blackmailed Mendax? It's all Mr B.'s FAULT for trying to sneak off to Gusty Bay without us!"

"So it is," agreed Old Noshie. "I don't feel at all guilty now. If we do something bad, it's only because he hurt our feelings."

3

The Seaside

There was terrible confusion at the vicarage next morning, with the Babbercorns and Mr Snelling trying to leave for their holidays at the same time. Mr Babbercorn and Alice had borrowed the vicar's car to drive down to Gusty Bay. Mr Babbercorn was loading it with nappies, buckets and spades and picnic baskets, until it seemed about to burst.

Mr Snelling was taking a taxi to the station, where he would catch his train to the airport. He was very flustered and nervous – he had not been away for years, and his ancient luggage was so mouldy that Mendax had made him buy a new suitcase.

Old Noshie and Skirty Marm jumped and laughed and turned somersaults, and got in everybody's way.

"I thought you said you were having a holiday

too," said Mr Babbercorn. "Don't you have any packing to do?"

"We've done it!" said Old Noshie happily.

The young curate had been very busy for the past few weeks, and he had not had time to investigate the witches' holiday plans properly. Now, he looked at them very seriously over the top of his glasses.

"Noshie and Skirty," he said, "I'll tell you the truth – I'm worried about this holiday of yours. It was very kind of Mendax to lend you the money for it, but I'm not sure you can pretend not to be witches for a whole two weeks!"

Alice laughed. "You worry too much, Cuthbert – it'll do the witches good to go off on their own for a change!"

"I'm trusting you both to remember all your promises," Mr Babbercorn said. "No magic, no tricks, no eating mice, no throwing squirrels at each other—"

"No SQUIRREL-CHUCKING?" Old Noshie was disappointed. "That's not fair!"

"It's the kind of thing that scares humans," said Mr Babbercorn, "quite apart from what it does to the squirrels. And it's very unkind to scare people on their holidays. Remember, witches – I'm trusting you to behave!"

Alice strapped Thomas into his car-seat. Then she kissed each witch. "Oh dear, I hate leaving you! Do have a lovely time, wherever you're going! And here's our address, in case you need us – the Sea Breeze Guest House, Railway Bridge Road, Gusty Bay."

"We'll send you a postcard," said Skirty Marm. She spoke cockily because her lip was wobbling. Saying goodbye to the Babbercorns felt awful. Old Noshie let out a sob and blew her nose on her sleeve. Both witches waved and waved as the car drove away down the lane. When it had gone, they stared forlornly at the place where it had been.

"I know we'll be in the same town," said Old Noshie, "but it won't be any good if we can't talk to them!"

The village taxi arrived at the gate for Mr Snelling.

Mendax gave him a lick and turned away to wipe his eyes with the end of his tail. "Have a marvellous time, dear vicar," he murmured. "And don't forget to put your reading glasses back in the right pocket!"

"I'll miss you, Mendax," the vicar said

tearfully. "If you or the witches need me, I'm at the Chateau Gateau, Normandy, France."

He drove off in his taxi, blowing his nose, and the witches and Mendax were left alone in a vicarage garden that suddenly seemed very quiet and sad.

Mendax was the first to recover. "At last!" he said briskly. "I thought we'd never get rid of them. Now I'll be able to work on that battle as long as I like – Time Machine or no Time Machine, I lose my thread when I have to rush back for dinner."

He picked up his bag of sandwiches. "If I don't come back, please look in the history books, to see how I died. It's bound to be SPECTACULAR."

The past and future hero of Fungus Gulch made his way towards the shed.

Old Noshie and Skirty Marm waited at the vicarage until it was dark – they were travelling by broomstick and did not want any human to see them. When the moon had risen in the clear sky, and all the fields were cloaked in blackness, they mounted their brooms in one of the open belfry windows.

It was some time since they had made a long journey by broom. Skirty Marm checked the radio-switches, which would enable them to talk to each other during the flight. Old Noshie checked the supply of Jammy Dodgers.

"Right!" said Skirty Marm. "Brooms – we're heading east, to the town of Gusty Bay!"

With screams of triumph they soared out into the night.

Although the witches did not like hot weather, they found that a warm summer night was perfect for flying. The gentle breezes stroked their rags and cooled their leathery skin. They enjoyed looking down at the sleeping farms and villages below.

After two hours in the air, they landed in a wood to eat their biscuits.

"It's nice to be flying again," said Old Noshie. "Broomsticks are a lot cheaper than trains."

"And it's nice to be free witches," Skirty Marm said thoughtfully. "Not having to worry about being GOOD all the time. Not having to ask Mr B. every time we want to cast a tiny spell!"

"If we're having a holiday from being good," said Old Noshie, "we can play tricks and have

154

laughs and hurl squirrels as much as we like – Mr B. and Alice won't even know!"

This was a very exciting idea, and it put both witches into a frisky mood. Skirty Marm started the holiday-from-goodness by making her dribble bright blue and spitting on cars. Old Noshie terrified some humans in a pub by suddenly flashing her green face at an upstairs window. Skirty Marm magicked away a policeman's clothes and left him shouting furiously in his underwear. This made them shriek with laughter.

"Cor, this is as good as Hallowe'en!" cried Old Noshie.

They decided to halt the naughtiness when they got close to Gusty Bay. As Skirty Marm pointed out, "We don't want to attract too much attention or Mr B. will notice something."

They flew over the ridge of a steep hill, and both cried, "OOH!"

Ahead of them lay the black rooftops of Gusty Bay, and beyond them –

"The SEA!" whispered Old Noshie.

For several minutes they hovered on their brooms in silence. They had never before seen how smooth and silver a moonlit sea can be.

This was far more beautiful than Slime Regis.

"The water doesn't shout here," said Skirty Marm. "It just sings and sighs!"

The small town of Gusty Bay was very dark and quiet, but the witches saw enough of it to be enchanted. There were coloured fairy-lights along the seafront and on the pier. Large seagulls pecked on the smooth sand. There was a delicious smell of old shellfish.

"We'll take a proper look tomorrow," said Skirty Marm, "when it's light."

Old Noshie yawned noisily. "Where shall we sleep, Skirty?"

"Under the pier looks cosy," said Skirty Marm.

They landed their brooms on the beach. The sand under the creaky wooden pier was damp and covered with clumps of smelly wet seaweed. Old Noshie sat down on it and popped a piece into her mouth.

"Yum – this is lovely!"

Skirty Marm settled herself comfortably against a pillar of wet wood, covered in greenish slime. "Save some for breakfast. Tomorrow's going to be a very busy day!"

*

The witches woke suddenly next morning, when a large wave broke right over their feet.

"Drat!" complained Skirty Marm, sitting up on the sand. "My stockings are soaked!"

Old Noshie had been dreaming about Noah's Ark. She was very relieved to find that the whole world was not flooded.

"We'd better put on our human clothes," she said, "before someone sees us!"

Both witches looked around with great interest. The day was grey and rather blustery, with a hint of rain. Above the beach, the shops on the promenade were starting to open – a lady in a pink overall was hanging rubber rings and coloured buckets outside the door of her café. There was a smell of salty dampness.

"Gorgeous weather!" Skirty Marm said happily. She opened the Tesco carrier bag that held her luggage and took out the strange collection of clothes she wore when she needed to disguise herself as a human old lady. Old Noshie covered her green face with white make-up and put on a brown wig instead of her usual blue one. Skirty Marm hid her purple hair under a woolly hat like a tea-cosy, and her fizzing red eyes behind a pair of sunglasses. In a few minutes, the two witches were transformed into two rather bonkers-looking old humans. All signs of witchiness – brooms, musty rags and pointed hats – were safely hidden under a huge clump of seaweed.

"Let's have something special to EAT!" cried Old Noshie. The smells from the café were making her stomach rumble.

"Good idea," said Skirty Marm. She picked up the smart human handbag, which one of her friends from the Old Folks' Drop-In Club had kindly given her, and checked the bundle of Mendax's human money. Both witches were in high holiday spirits. It was still early, and not many humans were about. They went into the café on the promenade and had an enormous breakfast of fried eggs, chips, tomato ketchup, chocolate cake and ice cream, all on the same plate. The lady in the shop was surprised to meet two old ladies with such huge appetites. She was even more surprised when these old ladies bought two rubber rings (one blue, one red with spots) and two fancy plastic spades.

"You won't get much digging done today," she said. "It looks like rain."

"Oh, I DO hope so!" cried Old Noshie. She

thought her spade was so beautiful, she tied it round her neck with a piece of string.

Large spots of rain were falling by the time the witches came out of the shop. Strangely, the humans did not seem to like this weather, and the beach was deserted.

"What shall we do next, Skirt?" asked Old Noshie.

Skirty Marm thought hard. "We could go and spy on Mr B. and Alice," she suggested.

"Great!" cried Old Noshie. "*Heeheehee* – wouldn't they be AMAZED if they knew?"

There was a map of Gusty Bay on the promenade. Skirty Marm, who was good at reading maps, looked for Railway Bridge Road. Old Noshie, who was useless with maps, bought two Mars Bars from a nearby sweetshop, to keep them going. Very happy and excited to be on their first human holiday, the witches set off through the town.

Railway Bridge Road, as you might have guessed, had a railway bridge at one end, and the station at the other.

"Goodness, how POSH!" said Skirty Marm.

The Sea Breeze Guest House was a narrow grey house, with a small front garden and a notice on the door that said "Vacancies".

Old Noshie grabbed Skirty's arm. "Look! I can see them!"

Through the hedge in the front garden, it was possible to see into the dining room. Mr Babbercorn, Alice and Thomas were sitting at a table in the window. Mr Babbercorn was eating a bowl of cornflakes, and Alice was sharing her toast with Thomas. The witches ducked behind the hedge so they would not be seen – this was important, since Mr Babbercorn kept looking out of the window at the grey sky.

"Let's follow them," said Skirty Marm. "They've been here before, so they must know all the nice things to do!"

The witches ate their Mars Bars while they waited for the Babbercorns to finish their breakfast. Presently, the front door of the guest house opened. Shaking with giggles, the witches kept out of sight, behind the dustbins of the house next door. Alice was pushing Thomas in his buggy. The whole family was wearing bright shorts and T-shirts and big raincoats. The unfamiliar sight of the curate without his dog-collar made the witches almost hysterical. Old Noshie had to stuff her wig into her mouth to keep quiet.

"Perhaps it'll clear up later," they heard Mr Babbercorn say. "In the meantime, there's always the slide-show at the Town Hall."

"Oh, well," Alice said cheerfully, "it's better than getting wet."

"Pooh," grumbled Old Noshie. "I wanted them to go to the beach, or play a nice game of Nutty Golf!"

"CRAZY Golf, you old fool!" snapped Skirty Marm. "Do you want the whole world to guess that we're witches?"

Taking great care not to be spotted, they followed the Babbercorns to a large brown building in the middle of the town.

Skirty Marm read the notice outside – *Gusty Bay Town Hall – Slide-Show and Lecture, Today at 10am – Treasures of Italy.*

They were very pleased to find that it did not cost anything to get in.

"What a bargain!" said Skirty Marm happily.

The witches had never seen a slide-show. The big hall inside the building was very dark and nearly empty. A man was projecting brightly coloured pictures on to a white screen. Another man was talking on the platform. The Babbercorns settled at the front, and Old Noshie and Skirty Marm took two rather wobbly chairs near the back.

"Next," said the man on the platform, "possibly the most famous painting in the world – the Mona Lisa, painted by Leonardo da Vinci around the year 1508."

The witches looked with interest at the famous picture, and were a little disappointed that it was only a smiling lady with brown hair. They liked the slide of the Leaning Tower of Pisa much better.

"It began to lean to one side before it was even finished," explained the man on the platform. "Now, this bell tower is one of the wonders of the world."

"It's a BELL TOWER, just like our belfry!" whispered Skirty Marm, impressed.

"I'm glad our belfry doesn't lean over like that," Old Noshie said. "We'd keep sliding out of the windows!"

At the front of the hall, Thomas began to shout, in Babyspeak. "This is BORING! Take me away from this stupid place! I won't stop SHOUTING till you do!"

Mr Babbercorn and Alice did not know Babyspeak, but they understood Thomas's squawks only too well. They put on their raincoats and wheeled the buggy out of the hall. The witches ducked out of sight just in time. Back in the street, the Babbercorns immediately took their raincoats off again. While they had been indoors, watching the slides, the weather had changed. The grey clouds had blown away, leaving the sea and sky bright blue. The whole town gleamed in dazzling sunshine.

"How lovely!" Alice cried. "Let's go down to the beach!"

"Oh, no!" groaned Skirty Marm. "How can we go rainbathing in such DISGUSTING weather?"

Old Noshie did not reply. She had halted beside a large rubbish bin and was staring inside it with eyes and mouth gaping. Someone had thrown away a large brown bottle of NASTY MEDICINE.

Now, as every human knows, drinking someone else's medicine is a very DANGEROUS and STUPID thing to do – almost as bad as taking POISON. To witches, however, Nasty Medicine is a great treat. All it does is make them shockingly tipsy. In the past, Nasty Medicine had got Old Noshie and Skirty Marm into all sorts of trouble, and they had solemnly promised Mr Babbercorn that they would never touch another drop.

"I wish we hadn't made that promise!" Old Noshie sighed now.

"BUM to our promise!" cried Skirty Marm, very rudely. "We're on holiday!"

And (to the amazement of several passers-by) she snatched the bottle of Nasty Medicine out of the bin and took a deep swig.

4

Nutty Golf and a Terrible Donkey

Ten minutes later, Old Noshie and Skirty Marm were sitting in the gutter outside the Town Hall, singing loudly:

"Oh, I DO like to be beside the SEASIDE,

Oh, I DO like to be beside the SEA!

Oh, I DO like to peep inside a rubbish BIN

And find some lovely Nasty MED – I – CINE!"

Old Noshie's brown wig had slipped to one side, and Skirty Marm had her sunglasses on upside down. The other people in the street gave the witches some very funny looks, but they did not care. I am very sorry to say that they were disgracefully drunk.

"I've had an idea!" cried Old Noshie. She only had ideas when she had been at the Nasty Medicine, and they were never good ideas. "Let's have a swim!"

The two witches had agreed that they should only swim at night, when there was no danger of anyone seeing them. But that was when they were sober. With a slug of Nasty Medicine inside them, they completely forgot to be sensible.

"*Hahaha*! I'll race yer down to the beach!" yelled Skirty Marm, leaping to her feet.

The holidaymakers and shoppers of Gusty Bay were very alarmed to see what looked like two ancient ladies dashing through the streets, knocking aside anyone who got in their way. Cackling with laughter, the witches ran across the beach to their sleeping place under the pier.

Lots of people had come out to enjoy the beautiful weather, and the beach was crowded. Unknown to the witches, at the other end of the beach Mr Babbercorn and Alice were reading magazines in deck chairs, while Thomas slept in Alice's lap.

"Oh, this is wonderful!" sighed Mr Babbercorn. "I feel as if I haven't a care in the world. I must say, much as I love those witches, things are jolly peaceful without them!"

He would have been horrified if he had guessed what was happening in the damp, shadowy place under the pier. Old Noshie and

Skirty Marm were unpacking their swimming-sacks. They had made themselves these huge things out of the vicar's old shower curtains, which they had found in the shed. The design on the curtains was tropical, with palm trees and pineapples. The witches thought them incredibly smart.

By witch standards, their swimming-sacks were rather revealing. Their heads stuck out at the tops, and you could see nearly all their arms.

"Pretty daring!" giggled Old Noshie tipsily.

"But madly chic!" said Skirty Marm. "If we wore these at Slime Regis, the other witches would go as green as YOU!"

Old Noshie took off her wig, and tied a bin bag over her bald head.

"You'd better cover up your hair," she told Skirty Marm.

"Certainly not," said Skirty Marm, shaking her purple locks. "It's my best feature."

The two witches, in their tropical swimming-sacks, skipped across the sand down to the water's edge. When a wave ran over their toes, they squealed with delight – the sea at Gusty Bay was so much warmer and gentler than the rough sea at Slime Regis. Skirty Marm rushed in at

once and began to swim at top speed – in fact, at about fifty miles an hour, which made every other swimmer near her very frightened.

"Wait for me!" yelled Old Noshie. Sending up a tremendous fountain of spray, she zipped through the water after her friend.

From the shore, it looked as if two speedboats were going berserk. A small crowd began to gather on the sand, and a policeman at the other end of the beach decided to see what was causing the disturbance.

Mr Babbercorn looked up from his magazine. "What's happening over there?"

"Don't worry," Alice said. "It's not your responsibility this time – you're on holiday, and the witches are miles away."

"Hmmm." Mr Babbercorn was thoughtful. "You know, I can't relax – I have the strangest feeling that Old Noshie and Skirty Marm are nearer than we think!"

But before he could investigate, the crowd at the other end of the beach began to break up.

The witches were tired of swimming. Before the policeman could catch up with them, they scurried back to their seaweedy place under the pier and dried themselves by blowing on each other (Old Noshie unfortunately blew on Skirty Marm too hard, and several people nearby had their ice creams puffed right out of the cones). If they had not broken their promise about Nasty Medicine, the witches would have tried to behave, but now all they cared about was having a wild and wicked time.

"Let's try that Nutty Golf!" yelled Old Noshie.

Laughing and biffing each other, they stomped along the promenade to the Crazy Golf course. Old Noshie's make-up had washed off in the sea, and her face glowed like a green traffic

170

light. Skirty Marm had lost her woolly hat, and her hair looked like a clump of purple seaweed. People gasped and stared as these two strange old ladies charged past them – but the witches did not care.

The Crazy Golf course was about the size of a small playground. If you have ever played this game at the seaside, you'll know that people have to knock little balls through model castles and little railways and dragons' tails, with as few hits as possible. That is the whole point of the game. But the witches thought that was boring. To the astonishment of the other people who were playing, Old Noshie and Skirty Marm started whacking their golf balls into each other's mouths. When they were tired of this, Skirty Marm turned all the golf balls into little bombs – whenever anyone hit one, it exploded in a shower of stars. Several people screamed, and one lady fainted.

"OI!" shouted the man in charge. "What do you think you're doing? I'll have the law on you!" He dashed away to fetch the policeman.

Down on the beach, Mr Babbercorn said, "There's a crowd around the Crazy Golf now – maybe I'd better take a look."

Alice only smiled, and gave him a cup of tea from her Thermos flask. "For the last time, stop worrying. We're on holiday!"

The witches had not noticed the chaos they were causing.

"Well, that was a good laugh!" said Skirty Marm, skipping away from the Crazy Golf course before the policeman arrived. "These human holidays are BRILL! What shall we do next?"

"LOOK!" Old Noshie was staring down at the beach, where three grey donkeys were giving children rides on the sand. The witches had never had a donkey-ride, and they were very interested. By a stroke of luck, two donkeys were free. Skirty Marm paid for two rides (even though she was tipsy, she still did not trust Old Noshie with the human money they had borrowed from Mendax). Laughing tremendously, the witches jumped on the backs of their donkeys.

Skirty Marm's donkey was rather young and nervous, and as soon as it felt a witch on its back, it shot across the sand like a firework.

"WHEEE!" shrieked Skirty Marm, as people dived out of the way. "Mine's winning! Hurry up, Noshie!"

Old Noshie was having trouble with her donkey. It was old and fat, with dirty grey hair. If Old Noshie had been looking at its face, she would have seen the animal smiling to itself nastily. It trundled very slowly across the sand.

"Get moving, you smelly old thing!" Old Noshie shouted. "Or I'll turn you into a mouse and EAT you!"

"Oh no you WON'T!" snarled the donkey, to Old Noshie's astonishment.

Just as she was deciding that she must have imagined it, they passed above a small rock

pool, and she saw the donkey's reflection.

A clever witch can disguise herself as anything she likes, but she can't fool any kind of mirror. Her reflection will always show the truth. And the reflection of this donkey made Old Noshie's green face turn deathly pale. When she looked down into the rock pool, she saw the grinning, hideous face of MRS ABERCROMBIE.

Old Noshie was having a ride on the back of the ex-queen of all the witches – the evil old monster who had sworn to kill her!

"Fetch your friend!" growled the donkey. "I want to speak to you both!"

"Shh-tp bibblelibble—" mumbled Old Noshie. She was so frightened, this was all that came out.

When Skirty Marm trotted over, on the back of her real donkey, she found Old Noshie sober as a judge and shaking like a jelly.

"What's the matter with you?" she demanded. "You look as if you've seen a GHOST!"

"She HAS!" said the donkey that was Mrs Abercrombie.

As soon as Skirty Marm saw the reflection in the rock pool, she stopped being cocky. Like Old

Noshie, she turned pale. Unlike Old Noshie, however, she kept her head.

"It's all right, Nosh!" she said. "She hasn't got the Power Hat – she can't hurt us!"

"What does she want?" squeaked Old Noshie.

"Give the donkey-man another fifty pence," said Mrs Abercrombie. "I've got something important to say to you."

The man in charge of the donkeys was rather surprised when Skirty Marm got off her donkey, and said, "We'll have another go with this fat ugly one – but we only want to talk to it."

"Suit yourselves," he said. "It's your money. But watch out, because that one BITES!"

Old Noshie was very glad to get out of the saddle – it was not nice to think of sitting on the back of Mrs Abercrombie.

The donkey led them to a quiet place on the beach, behind a pile of deck chairs. Now that they knew it was the ex-queen in disguise, the witches took a proper look at its face. It had a filthy grey beard, and mean little eyes. When it grinned at them, they saw that its mouth was full of huge METAL TEETH.

"All right," Skirty Marm said, doing her best

to sound very tough and brave. "What's all this about?"

The donkey said, "I want that cat. Get me that cat, or I'll KILL you and your soppy human friends!"

Old Noshie burst into tears.

"The cat-slave Mendax has stolen something that belongs to ME!" said the donkey. Its mouth was foaming with rage, and the cruel expression on its face made both witches shudder. "Ever since you two made my POWER HAT burst into flames, I have been working to win it back!"

"That's impossible," said Skirty Marm. "It's nothing but ashes now!"

"NOW it is," the donkey said, with an unpleasant smile. "But not THEN. You're forgetting your history lessons. Long ago, before the Power Hat was made into the form of a hat, it was a tiny, glowing piece of rock from the Hills Before Time. I have been searching the past for that piece of rock so I can bring it back to the present, and make my Power Hat all over again – just as if you'd never interfered! I traced the Stone back to the BATTLE OF FUNGUS GULCH."

Suddenly and very nastily, the donkey that was Mrs Abercrombie scowled. "I nearly had it! It was in my hand! And then a Time Machine landed on my head and squashed me flat – I've still got the tyre-marks on my BUM!"

The witches gasped. Even Old Noshie understood why the ex-queen was now so angry. By an amazing coincidence, her wicked plan to win back her throne had been foiled by one of Mendax's visits to the Charge of the Pointed Brooms.

"Nobody can resist that Glowing Stone," the donkey said hungrily. "I saw the cat snatch it up, and rush off in a panic!"

"Cor, I'm not surprised!" croaked Old Noshie, her teeth chattering. "Poor old Mendax!"

Skirty Marm was frowning her thinking-frown. "But why have you come after US? If you're so clever, why can't you find Mendax yourself?"

This was obviously a very good question, because Mrs Abercrombie looked furious.

"Because the Glowing Stone has HIDDEN him behind a cloaking-spell!" her donkey-mouth spat out, in a shower of spit. "And my magic isn't strong enough to break it! I'm clever enough to travel through time without one of those stupid, new-fangled Time Machines – but I'm not advanced enough to find my stone."

"The Glowing Stone doesn't want you to find it," Skirty Marm said boldly. "It never liked you when it was a hat! Even far back in time, it thinks you STINK."

"It won't be able to defy me when it's back under my control!" Mrs Abercrombie said. "And you two are going to lead me to it! Tell me where that cat is hiding – before I KILL YOU ALL!"

"Oh, Skirty, what shall we DO?" wailed Old Noshie in terror, thinking of Mr Babbercorn and Alice and little Thomas, only a few metres away.

"Pull yourself together!" ordered Skirty Marm. "As long as Mendax has the sense to hold on to that stone-thing, this nasty old bag can't touch us!"

This made the disguised donkey even more furious. "I'll follow you two to the ends of the earth! I won't rest until I've had my REVENGE! That cat has STOLEN my property!"

"She can't do anything!" cried Skirty Marm.

"Come on, Noshie!"

She grabbed her quaking green friend by the wrist and dashed across the beach towards the pier. The donkey let out a great BREE-HA-HA-HA of rage (if you have ever heard a donkey, you will know how loudly they can scream) and tried to gallop after them. But she could not gallop fast enough.

Old Noshie and Skirty Marm grabbed their broomsticks and witch clothes from under the pier.

"Where are we going?" cried Old Noshie.

Skirty Marm leapt on to her broom. "Quick – we've got to get to Mendax before she does! And I bet I know where he is!"

5

The Chateau Gateau

As soon as the two witches were in the air and Gusty Bay was behind them, Skirty Marm flicked the radio switch on her broom.

"If Mendax was in a panic, he'd have run straight to Mr Snelling – thank goodness he's not at home or Mrs A. would have caught that soppy cat in a second! Tell your broom to fly to the Chateau Gateau, in France!"

Old Noshie was burbling, "Oh deary deary me! Deary me!" over and over again. "Deary dear deary—"

"Calm down at once!" ordered Skirty Marm sternly.

"Oh, Skirty!" cried Old Noshie, "I'm so frightened! She'll catch Mendax and get that stone and make the Power Hat all over again and KILL us and all our friends—"

"CALM DOWN!" yelled Skirty Marm. "We

have to keep our heads. As long as we can find Mendax before she does, we'll have that magic stone. Don't you DARE mess this up!"

It was her strictest voice. Scared as she was, Old Noshie stopped burbling and moaning and made a real effort to be calm. Skirty Marm was very brave, and Old Noshie always followed her in times of danger.

"Sorry, Skirty, I won't," she said humbly.

"We'd better keep radio-silence now," said Skirty Marm, "or Mrs A. will find us too easily."

Both witches turned off their radios. With the wind rushing and roaring in their ears, they flew at top speed across the Channel to France. After about an hour, they saw the rich green fields of Normandy below them. Another twenty minutes, and they were circling above the turrets of a huge, grand castle – the Chateau Gateau, where Mr Snelling was having his posh cooking holiday.

The Chateau was so splendid that Old Noshie almost forgot to be frightened. "Wow, it's like something out of a film! Doesn't the vicar get lost inside it?"

"He's not as SILLY as you are," Skirty Marm said crushingly. "Now, we'd better hide our brooms."

There were some thick bushes near where they had landed. The witches hid their brooms underneath them and scuttled across the velvety lawn to the castle. They crept up to all the windows, peeping inside them one by one. They saw a ballroom, a very grand dining room, and a sitting room full of rather spindly-looking gold chairs.

"I bet they hurt your bottom," said Old Noshie.

"Let's find the kitchens," said Skirty Marm, who was still being very brave and efficient. "Mendax will be wherever the vicar is – and the vicar will be wherever FOOD is!"

The kitchens were at the back of the Chateau Gateau. If the witches had not been so anxious about Mendax and Mrs Abercrombie, they would have stared through the huge windows for hours. There were rows of dazzling stoves, gleaming sinks and shining fridges. There were bowls and whisks and electric mixers, and great simmering pans. It was as big as Mrs Abercrombie's Palace kitchen on Witch Island, but about a million times cleaner, not to mention quieter. Nobody would have dreamt of shouting or biffing here.

A man in a white coat, with a tall white hat, was giving instructions to a class of about twenty-five people. Skirty Marm gave Old Noshie an excited pinch when she saw Mr Snelling among them. He was wearing a striped apron and a tall chef's hat. His round face was anxiously watching the door of a large oven.

The two witches turned themselves into mist, seeped through the open window, and crawled into a big wooden cupboard that ran along the whole length of the room. It was full of very large pots, and they were very cramped when they turned back into solid witches.

Now they could hear the loud voice of the man in white, who was the teacher of the cookery class.

"This is the principle of the perfect soufflé," he was saying bossily. "When you take your soufflés from the oven, they will have puffed up as light as a SIGH – they must rise far above the rim of the dish – tall and spongy, like a chocolate-flavoured CLOUD—"

"I can smell Mendax!" Skirty Marm whispered. Witches have a very sharp sense of smell. "He's here somewhere! Cat – stop hiding! This is an EMERGENCY!"

Out of the dark shadows in the cupboard, they heard a well-known mew.

"Is that you, Skirty?"

Both witches sighed with relief. They were in time – they had reached Mendax before Mrs Abercrombie.

"Of course it's ME," said Skirty Marm. "We knew we'd find you here!"

"You're in a lot of TROUBLE," Old Noshie said, not very helpfully.

From somewhere in the long cupboard, they heard a quavering moan of fear. "I know," Mendax said. "I got the shock of my life when my Time Machine landed on Mrs Abercrombie. Is she after me?"

"She'll probably be here at any moment," whispered Skirty Marm. "We've got to think what to do about that stone-thing – we can't let Mrs A. get it back, so she can make the Power Hat all over again!"

"I lost my head," Mendax admitted. "I was sure she was going to KILL me at once, and I wanted to see my dear vicar once more." His voice was broken by a sob. "He doesn't even know I'm here, but it comforts me to be near him."

Skirty Marm lit the end of her finger (something witches can easily do without hurting themselves) and held it up. The small black head of Mendax was sticking out of one of the enormous pots. He had something lumpy tied up in a dirty handkerchief and fastened to his collar. His green eyes were full of fear.

"Witches, what on earth shall I do?" he mewed. "You've got to help me!"

Even though this was a serious emergency, Skirty Marm could not help feeling rather glad that the snooty talking cat was actually begging her for help. She always enjoyed being in charge.

"Let's get out of here," she hissed. "Follow me!"

Fearfully, Mendax climbed out of his pot. Old Noshie, who was as scared as he was, kindly stroked his back. Skirty Marm peeped out of the cupboard and saw everyone in the class taking their puffy soufflés out of the ovens. She beckoned to the others and crawled out of the cupboard across the stone kitchen floor, towards a handy door. The three of them scuttled out of the door, and Old Noshie slammed it behind her.

In the kitchen, every single soufflé suddenly collapsed.

"Bother and blow! My masterpiece ruined!" grumbled Mr Snelling.

Outside, Mendax took the dirty handkerchief out of his collar and unfolded it.

Old Noshie and Skirty Marm gasped as their eyes were suddenly dazzled by a burst of silver light. The Glowing Stone lay in Mendax's paw, casting its eerie rays around the bushes where they were hiding.

For a long time, they stared at it in silence. There was something sharp and piercing about the light that was partly painful and partly delicious. Their brains felt large and vacant, like empty warehouses waiting to be filled.

"You can't stop looking and looking at it," Mendax whispered. "I just couldn't help picking it up and taking it with me!" He shuddered. "But witches – I can't tell you how scared I was when I found Mrs Abercrombie under my Time Machine!"

"I bet you wish you'd left that funny stone where it was!" said Old Noshie.

Mendax sighed, and shook his head. "If I'd just run away and left the Glowing Stone for Mrs Abercrombie, she would have used it to muck about with history, so that none of us would even have got born! We've got to stop her re-making the Power Hat, or we might as well have ourselves measured for coffins."

There was another long silence while they all stared at the Glowing Stone.

"Well, what are we supposed to DO with the smelly thing?" Old Noshie said crossly. "We can't keep it – we can't hide it—"

"Shhh!" Skirty Marm snapped. She pointed down at the earth, where a very small earwig was making its way between two fallen leaves. "You never know how Mrs A. will disguise herself. This earwig could be her!"

She blew on the palm of her hand, and it turned into a mirror. She held this up above the earwig. Its reflection showed that it was only an earwig.

"Cor, that's a relief!" said Old Noshie, popping it into her mouth.

"You should look on the bright side, Mendax," Skirty Marm said. "You really are a hero now. Never mind Fungus Gulch – this'll get you straight into the Witch Island history books."

Mendax sounded a little more cheerful. "Really? Why?"

"Well, you've saved them from having the old bag back as their queen, haven't you?" said Skirty Marm. "They'll THANK you for nicking that Time Machine now!"

Suddenly, the blue summer sky darkened. A cold wind sprang up, tossing the branches of the trees and stripping the leaves from the bushes where they were hiding. Old Noshie moaned and clutched Skirty Marm's arm.

On the smooth lawn of the Chateau, a speck of black appeared. As they watched, the speck grew and grew – from the size of a conker to the size of a small elephant. Before their terrified eyes, a writhing mass of black smoke slowly took the horrible shape of Mrs Abercrombie.

With shaking paws, Mendax wrapped the Glowing Stone in his handkerchief and tucked it back into his collar.

"We've got to get away!" squeaked Old Noshie.

"Quick, on your broom!" cried Skirty Marm.

"She'd catch your broom in a second and squash you like a fly," Mendax said. "We must run to the old stables where I parked the Time Machine!"

Not fifty metres away, the hideous black

shape of Mrs Abercrombie let out a screech that
shook the earth like thunder.

"GIVE ME MY STONE! YOU'RE ALL
DEAD ANYWAY! YOU'LL NEVER GET
AWAY FROM ME!"

Skirty Marm took a firm hold of Old Noshie's
wrist.

"Now or never!" whispered Mendax.

He dashed across the grass towards the old
stables behind the castle. The witches ran after
him, Old Noshie stumbling and wailing. Mrs
Abercrombie saw them and began to chase
them. It was like being chased by a

thunderstorm. Panting for breath and scared half out of their wits, Mendax and the witches hurtled into the stables and threw themselves at the Time Machine.

"Where? Where?" mewed Mendax, his paws hovering over the controls.

"GIVE ME MY STONE!" Mrs Abercrombie was upon them.

Skirty Marm racked her brains – and remembered the lecture at the Gusty Bay Town Hall. "Italy, 1508!" she yelled. It was the first thing she could think of, though she had not a clue what it meant. Neither witch knew much about human history.

Mendax pulled the switch, and they were off.

A ride in a Time Machine is an extraordinary thing. You feel as if you are falling, falling, falling, with the centuries rushing through your hair, and all the noises of the years babbling around you.

They landed, with a tremendous jolt, in brilliant sunshine.

"Phew!" said Skirty Marm. "She'll never find us here!"

Meanwhile, back in Gusty Bay, Mr Babbercorn

and Alice were enjoying beautiful weather. They had spent a whole, lazy day on the beach, and were making their way back to the Sea Breeze Guest House, feeling very happy and sandy and pleasantly tired.

"I'm sorry I was fussing this morning," Mr Babbercorn said to Alice. "I couldn't stop worrying about the witches, but now I feel I've really got away from it all."

"The newspaper says the weather's going to be gorgeous," Alice said cheerfully. "Thomas will be as brown as a little nut when we get home!"

Mr Babbercorn chuckled. "And we won't have to sit through another of those lectures in the Town Hall!"

He would have been very surprised if he could have seen the changes that had come over the lecturer's box of slides. Next time it rained, the audience would hear about the peculiar things that had happened in Northern Italy, back in 1508. They would see pictures of the *Upright* Tower of Pisa, and the world's most famous painting – the MONA NOSHIE.

6

The Mona Noshie

The witches and Mendax lay in the hot sun, weak with relief that – so far – Mrs Abercrombie had not followed them. Mendax was the first to recover. He jumped out of the Time Machine. His voice had almost returned to its usual coolness.

"Listen, witches – I'm very sorry I got into such a panic. It was really very decent of you to come to the Chateau Gateau and take me away. I would have hated anything bad to happen to dear Mr Snelling." He smoothed his whiskers and patted the bulging handkerchief tucked into his collar. "Now, we must find somewhere safe to hide this stone."

Skirty Marm was trying to work out all kinds of complicated things to do with Time. "Shouldn't you put it back where it was, at Fungus Gulch?" she asked.

Mendax shook his head. "I've already thought of that. Mrs Abercrombie will go back and snatch it. She can only muck about with history if she has the Stone, so we have to hide it where she can't possibly find it. Then we'll get born, and the Power Hat will get burned, and things will be just the same."

"Easier said than done," Skirty Marm said. "What do you think, Noshie?"

"Eh?" Old Noshie had not heard a word of this. She was staring around with eyes like saucers.

They were in a grove of little olive trees, gnarled and twisted like gnomes. Beautiful fields stretched around it, shimmering in the heat. Below them, in the distance, they saw a magnificent city, full of sparkling white buildings.

"How exquisite!" purred elegant Mendax. "Florence in the early sixteenth century – at the very height of the Italian Renaissance!"

"What are you talking about?" Old Noshie asked crossly. "Speak Hinglish!"

Mendax sniffed haughtily. "I wouldn't expect an uncultured witch like you to appreciate this experience, but let me tell you, many a human would give their eye-teeth to be here!"

"Well, I'd give my eye-teeth and my EAR-teeth to get away from here," said Old Noshie. "I don't see what's so great about being chased by an evil fat monster!"

Skirty Marm had a little more feeling for culture than her green friend. "Maybe we'll find somewhere good to hide the Glowing Stone," she said. "Mendax, is there any way we can take a look around? We left our brooms in France."

"Pooh!" swore Old Noshie, who had forgotten this.

"There's a travel-button on the Time Machine," Mendax said, jumping back into the driver's seat. "Let's take a little tour and soak up the atmosphere." He pressed a button neatly with his paw. The dashboard opened and a steering-wheel popped up. The Time Machine soared into the warm sky, and the witches leaned rather dangerously out of their seats to gape at the wonderful view.

"Look!" shouted Old Noshie, "There's that broken bell tower we saw in the Town Hall!"

The Time Machine was circling gracefully above the famous Leaning Tower of Pisa. Because they lived in a bell tower themselves, the witches were very interested in this tall white tower, leaning to one side.

"It looks a bit windy," Skirty Marm said. "We'd need two pairs of bloomers in the winter if we had to live up there!"

"I think it's great!" cried Old Noshie. "Can't we stop and have a proper look? Oh, PLEASE!"

"If we stay in the air too long, it'll be easier for Mrs A. to spot us!" Skirty Marm pointed out. She was just as keen to examine the strange tower, which looked very much like the

ramshackle buildings of Witch Island.

Mendax landed the Time Machine on the wide open space in front of the Leaning Tower. This was hundreds of years before the invention of the aeroplane, and the people of Pisa were very frightened to see the Time Machine appearing out of the air above them. They were even more frightened when they saw its passengers. A noisy crowd gathered to stare at them – but from a long way off.

"*Heeheehee*! Look at their BONKERS CLOTHES!" yelled Skirty Marm.

They had never seen pictures of the clothes worn by humans in olden times and thought these were hilarious.

"The men are wearing STOCKINGS!" laughed Old Noshie. "And their hats look like CABBAGES! Hahahaha!"

"Oh, do pull yourselves together," Mendax muttered crossly. "Have you no feeling for history?"

Old Noshie climbed out of the Time Machine and looked up at the Leaning Tower.

"I don't like it, Skirt. It makes me ever so giddy."

A brilliant idea came to Skirty Marm. "I

know – let's STRAIGHTEN it! Won't they be pleased?"

"Are you crazy?" Mendax gasped indignantly.

But Skirty Marm was already standing beside Old Noshie. Witches are incredibly strong and all they had to do was push hard, with both hands. Before long, the Leaning Tower of Pisa was standing up straight. The people of Pisa screamed with terror. Also with anger, because the Tower was already a popular tourist attraction – and who would come to visit the Upright Tower of Pisa?

"You'll thank us for this later!" Skirty Marm shouted at them. She got back into the Time Machine. "Come on, Noshie. Humans are so ungrateful sometimes."

"You've destroyed one of the wonders of the world," spat Mendax. "I hope you're SATISFIED!"

Before the angry citizens of Pisa could rush at them, the Time Machine took off again. The tower – now standing as upright as an exclamation mark – fell away behind them.

"I'm hungry," Old Noshie complained. "I keep thinking about that puffy chocolate thing the vicar was making!"

Mendax sighed. "I have some sandwiches in the glove compartment. I suppose we had better stop for a rest."

They were above the city of Florence now. Mendax landed the Time Machine in farmland on the outskirts and hid it carefully in a haystack, not wanting to attract any more attention. Unfortunately, they looked extremely odd to the humans they met. The witches were still wearing their human old-lady disguises from Gusty Bay. And green skin and purple hair look odd practically everywhere.

In the narrow, crowded streets of the city, they were careful to stick to the darkest places. Eventually, when their stomachs were rumbling terribly, they found a deserted alley. Skirty Marm took Mendax's sandwiches out of her coat pocket and divided them into three rather small portions.

"Huh! Fish-paste again!" she grumbled, with her mouth full.

Suddenly, a door opened in the alley. Out came an old man, with a long white beard. At first, he was shocked to see what were obviously two witches – as all humans are. But slowly, he seemed to become fascinated with the green face of Old Noshie. He stared at her with very bright, sharp eyes, until Old Noshie, began to get annoyed.

"He's after my sandwiches! Go away, you nasty man! Shoo!"

The old man gabbled something at them in a strange language.

"Good gracious!" mewed Mendax, astonished. "It must be because I'm wearing the Glowing Stone – I can understand him!" He listened for a moment. "He says he's a painter. The lady he was going to paint is late – and anyway, he doesn't want her any more. He wants to paint Old Noshie instead."

"What colour?" asked Skirty Marm.

"I like being green!" shouted Old Noshie.

Mendax rolled his eyes impatiently. "Noshie, must you be such a PEASANT? He wants to paint a picture of you!"

"Of ME?" Nobody had ever wanted a picture of Old Noshie before, and she was flattered – particularly when she saw Skirty Marm's jealous scowl. "All right!"

"He could be Mrs A. in disguise!" Skirty Marm muttered. "We'll all be killed, just because you're a SHOW-OFF!"

"Bum to you!" smirked Old Noshie.

Mendax was also jealous – he was very vain. "I can't think why he wants a painting of a HAIRLESS SPROUT," he sniffed, "but he says he'll give us some food, so let's go inside."

The old man seemed excited. He led them into his house, and said something to a lady. (Skirty Marm remembered to check the lady's reflection in her mirror-hand.) The lady began to spread a table with cakes and pies and delicious bread. Then it was Old Noshie's turn to be annoyed – she could not eat anything because the old man made her sit still to have her portrait painted. Old Noshie was a fidgety witch, and she was hungry. She looked at the food so longingly that Skirty Marm forgave her for being painted and stored a couple of pies in her pocket to eat later.

At last, the painting (that should have been the Mona Lisa, and was now the Mona Noshie) was finished. The lady came back and said something to the old man.

Mendax translated. "She says there's a cardinal come to sit for his portrait." He stiffened suddenly. "But the old man says he's not expecting anyone. I don't like the sound of that!"

Taking care to stay hidden, Skirty Marm ran to the top of the stairs. At the bottom stood a stout man in a bright red dress. He looked very important, and his hands were covered with glittering rings. But Skirty Marm saw his reflection in her mirror-hand – and nearly screamed aloud. She rushed to her friends.

"It's HER! We've got to get out!"

"What about my PIE?" moaned Old Noshie.

The other two ignored her. Skirty Marm grabbed Noshie's hand, and Mendax pulled at her coat with his teeth. Together they jumped out of the window, just as the heavy footsteps of

Mrs Abercrombie were heard on the stairs. They ran out of the alley and quickly hid inside an old barrel.

It had been a very close shave. They stayed in the barrel until it got dark, to have a better chance of escaping without Mrs Abercrombie seeing them. Mendax discovered that he could instruct the Glowing Stone to hide them from the humans, but Mrs Abercrombie was horribly clever, and Mendax wasn't absolutely sure the Stone could conceal them from her.

At the dead of night, very scared and very tired, they finally returned to the haystack where they had parked the Time Machine.

"I want to go HOME!" wailed Old Noshie.

"Stop that grizzling!" spat Mendax crossly. "We can't!"

"Hang on!" cried Skirty Marm. "I've had an idea! Jump in, both of you!" She leapt into the driver's seat.

"I can't imagine what you're doing, and I don't care," Mendax said, fastening his seat belt. "If either of you survive me, I'd like a very quiet funeral. The dear vicar might like to have me stuffed."

Skirty Marm – very excited – was turning the

dials on the dashboard. Then she pulled the switch, and they were thrown back into the rushing stream of Time.

After a while, they halted. To the amazement and horror of Mendax, they were back in the garden shed at the vicarage.

"You IDIOT!" he groaned. "She'll find us in about thirty seconds! We're all going to DIE! And by the way, you owe me money – OW!"

Skirty Marm had pushed the small cat roughly out of the Time Machine. She shoved Old Noshie out after him, and jumped out herself. Suddenly, there was a tremendous clap of thunder that made the whole shed shake as if it were made of tissue paper.

Mrs Abercrombie had crashed down in the vicarage garden.

Old Noshie bellowed with fear and hid her face in her hat. Skirty Marm, however, stayed calm. She plucked the handkerchief out of Mendax's collar and shut it in the glove compartment of the Time Machine. Then she did something very brave – possibly the bravest thing she had ever done in the whole of her brave career. She turned the dials on the dashboard to their highest settings, pulled the switch and jumped out of the Time Machine a split second before it vanished into thin air.

In the stunned silence that followed, Mendax sat up, rubbing his shoulder. Old Noshie finally dared to take her face out of her hat. There was nothing but dusty empty space where the Time Machine had been.

Skirty Marm was very pale. Sparks flew from the ends of her purple hair, and it stood out like a brush. "I've sent the Glowing Stone heaven-knows-WHERE, and heaven-knows-WHEN!" she said breathlessly. "It will whirl round in SPACE for ever – she'll have to go through the whole UNIVERSE with a comb to find it now!"

"That was exceedingly bright of you, Skirty Marm," said Mendax. "And under the circumstances, you can keep the money."

Old Noshie began to tremble. A black, conker-sized speck was hovering in the corner of the shed, above the lawnmower. Once again, as they watched, it swelled and writhed and took the disgusting form of Mrs Abercrombie.

The lightning flashed and the thunder rolled, until the skies above Tranters End seemed about to split open. The ex-queen of the witches already knew what had happened to the

Glowing Stone. She was so furious that her skin was smoking all over.

"I WILL HAVE MY HAT!" she roared. "AND WHEN I GET IT BACK, I WILL HAVE MY REVENGE! AAAARGH!"

There was a deafening crash. The witches and Mendax were lifted off their feet and landed in a hot shower of dust and soil. When they had stopped coughing and spluttering, they gazed around them in astonishment.

A sweet and peaceful silence had fallen upon the village of Tranters End. But there was no garden shed at the vicarage any more – no rowing machine, no lawnmower, no deck chairs, no old tins of paint. Old Noshie, Skirty Marm and Mendax were sitting on the bald, blackened piece of earth where it had been.

"Blimey!" murmured Skirty Marm, very impressed. "She was so angry, she EXPLODED!"

Mendax staggered up on shaking paws. "I think I'll put the kettle on."

Old Noshie sniffed. "I wish Mr B. and Alice were here. I don't even care if they're cross about the shed. I just want to see them, to make sure they're safe!"

And at that moment, Mr Babbercorn's voice called from the house, "Witches! Mendax! Good grief – where's the shed?"

There, at the back door, was Mr Babbercorn, with Alice behind him and Thomas in her arms. They all looked very brown and healthy. The weedy curate had grown a little fatter.

"But what are they doing here?" wondered Skirty Marm. "They're not due back for another two weeks!"

"You must have set the Time Machine to the wrong day when we came back," Mendax said. "And I'm glad you did – if the Babbercorns are home now, that means my dear Mr Snelling will be back this afternoon!"

The three of them waved to Mr Babbercorn and Alice and began to hurry towards the house.

"You know," Old Noshie said, "I think being without us has done them a lot of good. Look how pleased they are to see us again!"

"They've missed us!" Skirty Marm said proudly. "Maybe we were wrong to follow them on their holiday. Maybe we should let them go away by themselves again next year." She sighed. "I'm sorry we had to leave those rubber rings at Gusty Bay!"

"I'll let you wear my spade sometimes," offered Old Noshie, who still had this beautiful object tied round her neck. "After all, you were very brave."

Mr Babbercorn had had such a delightful holiday that he was only a little irritated about the shed. Mr Snelling – who had had a marvellous time at the Chateau Gateau – did not mind either.

"I'm glad that rowing machine's gone," he declared. "It made me feel guilty every time I went in there."

The witches decided not to tell Mr Babbercorn about Gusty Bay and the Nasty Medicine – but they did tell the whole story to Chancellor Badsleeves, their old friend, who was now the leader of Witch Island. As Skirty Marm had predicted, she forgave Mendax for stealing the Time Machine. The explosion of Mrs Abercrombie had caused great rejoicing amongst the witches, and the Chancellor solemnly declared a National Explosion Day every year, to be celebrated with fireworks. She also promised to send a crack Time-squad to clear up the bits of human history the witches had damaged.

Old Noshie did not mind too much about her portrait disappearing from history.

"But they needn't have changed everything back!" she declared. "I still think that tower looks better when it's STRAIGHT!"

Broomsticks in Space

For Bertie and Archie

1

Marrow Madness

Skirty Marm landed her broomstick in the lane beside Blodge Farm and took a large, grubby piece of paper out of her hat. This was a list of names, and each name had a row of numbers beside it.

"Mrs Blenkinsop," read Skirty Marm. "Her marrow was forty-eight and a half centimetres, last time we looked. That's three whole centimetres bigger than ours."

Old Noshie had landed rather clumsily in the hedge. She struggled out of a clump of thorns. "Perhaps it's stopped growing," she said hopefully. "Perhaps it'll start shrinking soon, until it's just a tiny little courgette."

Once a week, all through this long, warm summer, the two witches had flown round the village of Tranters End, measuring every single vegetable marrow. There were no less than fifteen of these green monsters, lying in gardens and vegetable patches like vast, overgrown cucumbers. Marrows are not very exciting to eat, but the villagers were not growing them for food. They were all after the Marrow Cup – a silver cup, given every year at the Flower Show to the person who had raised the biggest marrow in Tranters End.

This year, for the first time, Old Noshie and Skirty Marm had entered the competition. They were both very proud of the fine, fat marrow they were growing in the vicarage garden. Old Noshie wanted to win that silver cup more than anything in the world. She lay awake at night, fretting over the sizes of all the other marrows in the village. Skirty Marm pretended not to care so much, but it had been her idea to measure their rivals' marrows.

Nobody in Tranters End was at all startled when they saw two determined witches flying from garden to garden with their tape-measure. Though it is far from usual to find two genuine witches, dressed in dusty rags and pointed hats, in a quiet English village, Old Noshie and Skirty Marm had become part of the scenery there. There had been some fuss when they first arrived, and several hair-raising magic incidents, but the villagers were now quite used to having a pair of witches living in the belfry of their church. They had even stopped thinking Old Noshie and Skirty Marm looked odd. Though of course, they did. Witches are not at all like humans – as you would know at once if you ever saw one. Their skin has a leathery toughness, and their hair is like the hard string used for tying parcels.

Old Noshie was a plump, bumbling sort of witch, with bright green skin that glowed in the dark. Her head was as bald as an egg, and she wore a blue wig to keep it warm. Skirty Marm was a skinny witch, with grey skin, purple hair, and red eyes that shot out sparks when she was angry.

The two witches had found Tranters End by mistake. It had happened nearly four years ago, at Hallowe'en. Old Noshie and Skirty Marm had been banished from Witch Island for singing a rude song about their wicked queen, Mrs Abercrombie. When they first came to the belfry, the two exiled witches had been very homesick. Nowadays they lived very happily underneath the deafening church bells.

Things had not always been so happy, how-ever. For their first couple of years with the humans, Skirty and Noshie had been at war with the terrible MRS ABERCROMBIE. The ex-queen had done everything she could to destroy Old Noshie and Skirty Marm. She had plenty of reasons to hate them.

First, they had helped to bring about the Witch Island Revolution, which finally threw the evil queen off her throne.

Second (and worst of all), they had stolen the POWER HAT. This was an extraordinarily powerful witch's hat, two metres tall, with an everlasting candle burning at its point. Nobody knew all its secrets, but this Hat was the very heart of Mrs Abercrombie's power. Without it, she was nothing more than a very clever, very wicked and very ancient witch. With the Power Hat, she was the strongest witch in the world.

After Old Noshie and Skirty Marm stole the Hat, Mrs Abercrombie had laid all kinds of evil plans to snatch it back and had sworn never to rest until the Power Hat was hers once more.

In the end, the Power Hat had been Mrs Abercrombie's undoing. After one desperate battle it had burst into flames and vanished in a cloud of ash. Still Mrs Abercrombie refused to give in. She knew that before it had become a hat, this strange magic article had been a small piece of stone, with an eerie, silvery glow. Who should know better than Mrs Abercrombie, the very witch who had made the Hat? Yet again, she had refused to admit defeat. She had gone back in a Time Machine to capture the Glowing Stone and start all over again.

Then Skirty Marm had rescued the Glowing Stone and sent it hurtling away into outer space. Mrs Abercrombie had been so furious, she had EXPLODED. Her rage and disappointment blew her into a million pieces, and (like a wicked old witch at the end of a fairy story) she was never seen again.

All this had happened nearly a year ago. Since then, free from the looming shadow of Mrs A., the two witches had enjoyed the happiest, most peaceful year of their lives. As Old Noshie said: "I don't even see her disgusting face in my nightmares any more!"

Back on Witch Island, Old Noshie and Skirty Marm were national heroines for blowing up the evil ex-queen. If they had fancied it, they could have returned in triumph as two very important witches in the government (the witches' new leader, Chancellor Badsleeves, was an old friend of theirs). But they could not think of leaving their human friends in Tranters End. The greatest of these friends was the young curate, Mr Cuthbert Babbercorn. They also loved his sweet wife, Alice – who had once been turned into a snail by Mrs Abercrombie – and the Babbercorn baby, Thomas, who was their godson. Next to the Babbercorns, the witches loved Mr Snelling, the plump and kindly vicar. Before they came to Tranters End, Old Noshie and Skirty Marm had known nothing about human friendship, or human love – so much kinder and deeper than the witch version. Now that they did know about it, they could never live on Witch Island. Chancellor Badsleeves often complained that they had been "ruined" by soppy human ways.

Old Noshie and Skirty Marm liked these soppy ways and were proud to have so many friends in the village.

One of these called to them now, from the garden of his bungalow. "Afternoon, witches!" It was Mr Fisher, their friend from the Old Folks' Drop-In Club. "Is it measuring-day again?"

"Hello, Mr Fisher," said Old Noshie. "We're measuring a day early this week because we're off today."

Both witches made important-yet-modest faces, and Mr Fisher cried, "I nearly forgot! It's your special visit to Witch Island! Well, I hope you have a wonderful time."

Skirty Marm was worried. "Do you think our marrow will be all right while we're gone?"

Mr Fisher was not entering for the Marrow Cup this year, so he was free to give the witches advice. "It'll be fine as long as it has enough water. The only things a marrow doesn't like are FROST and SNOW."

"Suppose there's a frost?" cried old Noshie in alarm.

Mr Fisher wanted to laugh, but politely turned it into a cough so he would not hurt the witches' feelings. "You won't get a frost in a lovely warm summer like this!"

Old Noshie and Skirty Marm had joined the Old Folks' Drop-In Club because they were over one hundred and fifty years old. This is very, very old for a human. But the kind and patient old people at the Club never forgot that one hundred and fifty is very, very young for a witch. Noshie and Skirty had also joined the Brownies, and felt quite at home playing and squabbling with the little girls.

Old Noshie squashed her green face between the slats of Mr Fisher's fence. "Everybody's marrow is bigger than ours. It's not fair. I do wish we could use just a tiny bit of magic!"

Skirty Marm snorted impatiently. "For the last time, you know we can't! If there's anything dodgy about our marrow, it'll be chucked right out of the Flower Show!"

"You know the rule," said Mr Fisher. "No

magic without Mr Babbercorn's permission."

"And he's never going to give us permission to CHEAT," said Skirty Marm. She sighed. There had been no major magic since the explosion of Mrs Abercrombie, and she could not help missing it a little. Skirty Marm had been top of her class at witch school, and winner of the Spellbinders' Medal for thirty-six years in a row. Mr Babbercorn allowed the witches to fly around the village on their brooms, and they occasionally cast very minor spells to unblock drains or mend fridges. But these were nothing to a witch who had once won the Transformation Cup by turning Old Noshie into a toadstool. Skirty Marm had to keep reminding herself that living without magic was better than living in fear of Mrs Abercrombie.

Old Noshie, always bottom of the class at school, had not missed magic nearly so much – until now. "Isn't there anything we can do to make our marrow grow?" she asked wistfully.

Mr Fisher kindly told them how to feed the marrow with sugared water and a piece of darning wool (he said this did not count as cheating), and added, "By the way – tell that Fancy-Pants talking cat to leave my roses alone!

I'm growing them for the Flower Show, not for Mr Mendax to give to his girlfriend!"

Old Noshie and Skirty Marm fell into a loud fit of giggles. Mendax was a talking cat who had been adopted by Mr Snelling. He had once been a cat-slave on Witch Island, sent by Mrs Abercrombie to spy on the witches. Though he was now a reformed character, the witches found it hard to forget his shady past. They thought it was very funny that this snooty, superior cat had fallen in love. Mendax had lost his heart to Gingersnap, the sister of the cat at the Post Office.

Skirty Marm sang, "Mendax and Gingersnap sitting in a tree – K-I-S-S-I-N-G!"

Old Noshie's marrow-fixated mind was already on the business of measuring. She led Skirty Marm through the gate of Blodge Farm and round the back of the large farmhouse to the vegetable patch. Mrs Blenkinsop's marrow lay under wire netting and looked depressingly enormous.

Old Noshie measured it, and her green lip wobbled. "Fifty centimetres!" she moaned.

Above them, a window flew open. From inside the house, Mrs Blenkinsop's voice

shouted, "Fifty-ONE centimetres, if you don't mind! You can measure all you like, but it won't stop my marrow winning the cup!" And she banged the window shut.

I'm very sorry to say that the two witches replied by sticking out their tongues and yelling, "BUM!"

Mr Babbercorn was beginning to worry that the Marrow Cup was not bringing out the best in the people of Tranters End. It had certainly not brought out the best in Old Noshie, usually such an easy-going witch. For the rest of that afternoon she got crosser and crosser as the rival marrows seemed to get bigger.

"Only six marrows smaller than ours," she said furiously when the measuring was over. "And Mrs Tucker's is a whole TWENTY centimetres bigger! It's not fair!"

Mrs Tucker kept the Post Office and General Shop and was also Brown Owl. The witches admired her very much, but Old Noshie was so jealous of the marrow that she wanted to spit on Mrs Tucker's washing – and she would have done, if Skirty Marm had not knocked her off her broomstick in the nick of time.

"I don't know what's got into you," Skirty said severely, when the two of them were back in their dusty belfry. "This is a very important day for us, and all you can think of is that stupid marrow!"

"The silver cup would look so great up here!" sighed Old Noshie. "I've cleared a special space for it, on top of my slug-box."

Skirty Marm gave her friend a quick biff on the nose to organize her thoughts. "Hurry up and get ready – we mustn't be late for the ceremony!"

The two witches and Mendax had been invited back to Witch Island for a Grand

Ceremony to honour them for the part they had played in Mrs Abercrombie's explosion.

"I wish they'd told us what sort of honour we're getting," said Old Noshie. "I hope it's a big FEAST!"

"You would," Skirty Marm said crushingly. "I'm hoping for a MEDAL. Or perhaps a TITLE – I've always fancied being a Dame of the Dustbin. Then I could sign my name 'Skirty Marm DD'."

Witches are not very tidy creatures, but Old Noshie and Skirty Marm made a special effort to look smart for this great occasion. Old Noshie polished her bald head before putting on her wig, and decorated her hat with a muddy lettuce. Skirty Marm felt very elegant in her new earrings, made of two old tea-strainers. They cleaned their broomsticks carefully and flew down to the vicarage garden.

Mr Babbercorn, Mr Snelling, Alice and Thomas were waiting to see them off. Mr Babbercorn held baby Thomas, and Alice held three paper bags.

"Just a snack to keep you going," she said, smiling. "Jam sandwiches for you two, and fish-paste for Mendax."

The vicar looked nervously at his watch. "Where is Mendax? That cat is always disappearing!"

"Here he comes," said Mr Babbercorn.

The small black cat strolled along the garden wall and dropped onto the lawn. He was humming to himself. His bright green eyes were dreamy, and there was a buttercup stuck in his collar. Old Noshie and Skirty Marm began giggling again.

"Am I late?" Mendax asked. "I was just saying goodbye to Gingersnap – sweet, artless little thing! How she blushed when she pressed this buttercup into my paw!"

"I dunno what you see in that cat," said Skirty Marm. "All she does is MEW!"

Mendax was offended. "I can still hold a conversation with ordinary cats, you know. And I find Gingersnap's innocence delightful. It does me so much good to talk to this simple village beauty and her honest brother!"

Mr Snelling bent down to kiss Mendax and to give him the small crash-helmet he had bought from a very expensive toy shop – the vicar spoiled his cat dreadfully. Mendax put on his helmet and settled in his basket on the back of Old Noshie's broomstick.

"Have a fantastic time, all of you!" said Mr Babbercorn. "You deserve to be honoured for your bravery." His eyes were very serious behind his glasses. "I know I can trust you to behave. Remember your promise to stay off the NASTY MEDICINE."

The witches looked rather sulky. As every human knows, it is STUPID and DANGEROUS to drink someone else's medicine, but for witches Nasty Medicine is a treat – all it does is make them disgustingly tipsy. Nasty Medicine

had got Old Noshie and Skirty Marm into all sorts of trouble in the past, but that did not stop them liking it.

"Couldn't we have just a little drop?" asked Skirty Marm. "Everyone else will be drinking – it'd be RUDE not to!"

"Absolutely not," Mr Babbercorn said firmly.

"You're supposed to be setting an example to the younger witches," Mr Snelling reminded them.

"Huh!" muttered Old Noshie. "They'll be too drunk to notice!"

Mr Babbercorn was a thin, pale, weedy young man – but he was the only person who could keep the witches in order. "I'm sorry, witches," he said, very kindly but very firmly. "No Nasty Medicine. Remember, you live with humans these days."

"Come home soon!" cried Alice. "Don't get so famous on Witch Island that you forget us!"

The witches could never do that. Their sulks melted away as they kissed and hugged the humans. Then, in the soft afternoon sunshine, they mounted their brooms.

2

Explosion Day

After two hours of hard flying (with a short break in Norway to eat their sandwiches), the witches and Mendax noticed a change in the air. It became colder, with a lashing wind and a dampness that seemed to seep into the marrow of their bones. The stormy sea was black beneath a threatening grey sky. The witches rammed their hats on tighter and put their brooms into second gear. Ahead of them, a black, jagged, sinister heap of rocks loomed through the mist.

Old Noshie and Skirty Marm cackled with delight. Although they had picked up many human tastes (for instance, electric light, decent biscuits) they still missed the ghastly weather of their old home.

"Mmmm, just SMELL it!" cried Skirty Marm as the familiar stink of bad eggs began to waft up from the rocks below.

Mendax, swinging giddily in his basket, shivered. His memories of Witch Island were not happy ones. In the dark days of Mrs Abercrombie, before slavery was made illegal, he had been a cat-slave. Many cats had been treated very cruelly, and Mendax had been beaten and starved by his drunken old owner.

The little cat forgot all this, however, when he saw the welcome that had been laid on for the Heroes of the Explosion. As the broomsticks circled above the palace beach, they all gasped.

A huge bonfire burned on the black sands. Hundreds of witches were crowded around it. As Old Noshie and Skirty Marm landed the brooms (careful not to squash anyone in the crowd) they were almost deafened by the loud cheers. Beneath this, they heard the deep and rasping notes of the Pock-horn – a witches' musical instrument, which looks rather like an enormous hot-water bottle made of metal. A group of witches held up a banner which said, "HAPPY EXPLOSION DAY, OLD NOSHIE AND SKIRTY MARM!" A group of former cat-slaves were chanting, "Men-DAX! Men-DAX! Men-DAX!"

"Dear me," murmured Mendax, wiping away a tear with his paw. "One is quite overwhelmed!"

A beaming, toothless witch pushed her way through the crowd.

"BINBAG!" yelled Old Noshie and Skirty Marm. Binbag was an old friend from school, and they were delighted to see her. Skirty Marm biffed Binbag's nose. Old Noshie knocked off Binbag's hat and jumped on it. Several witches nearby wept to see this touching reunion.

"This is our first National Explosion Day!" Binbag shouted, above the din. "We're going to have one every year – and it's all because of you!"

"Pooh, it was nothing!" mumbled Old Noshie, grinning and blushing dark green. Being hailed as a heroine was lovely and almost took her mind off the marrow.

The two witches and Mendax were escorted through the cheering crowd to the Meeting Cave, where the ceremony was to take place. Palace guards carried their broomsticks, Mendax's basket and the remaining sandwiches.

"Don't squash them," said Old Noshie. "I might fancy one later."

The Meeting Cave was a vast underground cavern, carved into the rock. It was packed with thousands and thousands of witches, all seated according to age and rank. I will quickly explain how you tell the age and importance of a witch. It's all in the STOCKINGS.

Up in the gallery of the Meeting Cave sat the YELLOW-STOCKINGS. These are baby witches, under the age of one hundred and still at school. In front of them were the young RED-STOCKINGS, who were between the ages of one hundred and two hundred – Old Noshie and Skirty Marm were Red-Stockings.

The front rows of the Meeting Cave were divided into two blocks. On the left-hand side sat the GREEN-STOCKINGS – that is, witches between the ages of two hundred and three hundred. On the right side sat the oldest and most powerful witches of all, the PURPLE-STOCKINGS.

Some of these witches were very old indeed. Mrs Abercrombie had been nearly a thousand, and though she had been one of the cleverest witches, she was not the oldest. Purple-Stockings are the kind of witches you read about in fairy stories. If you ever have a nightmare about a wicked witch, ten to one she'll be wearing purple stockings.

Under Mrs Abercrombie's evil rule, the old Purples kept cat-slaves and bullied the younger witches. The Revolution had changed all that by chucking out the queen and electing a popular Red-Stocking government. Nowadays, the Purples had far less power, and they were always grumbling about "fancy new-fangled ways". They did not think the Explosion of Mrs Abercrombie was a reason for celebration, and they were the only witches who did not cheer when Old Noshie and Skirty Marm were led on to the platform in the Meeting Cave.

It was very strange for Old Noshie and Skirty Marm. The last time they had stood in this cave, with everyone staring at them, they had been prisoners. Mrs Abercrombie had found them guilty of treason for singing the disgracefully rude song about her. She had stripped away their red stockings and banished them for a hundred years. Who could have imagined, on that terrible day, that the two disgraced witches would return in triumph?

There was a loud Pock-horn fanfare, and Chancellor Badsleeves entered. She was a stout witch, with short white hair and round glasses. Since the overthrow of Mrs Abercrombie, she had been the Chancellor of Witch Island. She was an old friend of Old Noshie and Skirty Marm's (she had lived in the cave next door), and she gave them a beaming smile as she held up her hand for silence. A hush fell upon the great Cave.

"Fellow-witches," said Badsleeves, "we are gathered here today to honour the three citizens who gave us EXPLOSION DAY. These two witches, and this cat, have beaten Mrs Abercrombie again and again. On the last occasion they sent the Glowing Stone into outer space, where the nasty old bag couldn't get her hands on it. They made her so furious, she Exploded. It is my great pleasure to reward them with the highest honours of our Island."

There was another Pock-horn fanfare. A Purple-Stocking palace guard brought in a ragged black cushion. Chancellor Badsleeves picked up a small medal, on a short silk ribbon.

"Step forward, MENDAX!"

Mendax stepped forward on shaking paws and bowed to the Chancellor. The freed cat-slaves, sitting at the front and sides of the cave, burst into ear-splitting mews.

"Mendax, for your bravery I hereby make you a KNIGHT OF THE NEWT." She hung the medal round his neck. "Arise, Sir Mendax, KN."

This ancient honour had never been given to a cat before. In their pride and joy, the cats began to swarm and shriek. Mendax was, for once, speechless. He gaped at the cheering cats, posed for photographs with the Chancellor, and slunk to the back of the platform in a state of shock. This was more wonderful than his

wildest dreams. In Latin (as Mr Snelling loved to point out), "Mendax" means "Liar", and this cat did tell some thumping lies – even he would never have dared to lie on such a magnificent scale as this.

Skirty Marm nudged Old Noshie excitedly. If Mendax was a Knight of the Newt, what did Badsleeves have in store for them?

"Step forward, OLD NOSHIE and SKIRTY MARM!"

The two witches stepped forward, feeling very awkward, and bowed to Badsleeves. The lettuce on Old Noshie's hat fell off and hit the Chancellor's foot.

"Noshie and Skirty," said Badsleeves, forgetting to be grand, "you outwitted Mrs Abercrombie until the old horror got so mad she Exploded. We can't thank you enough, and we're making you Dames of the Dustbin. But you expected that. We thought you deserved something extra – and then we remembered that Mrs A. had stripped you of your STOCKINGS."

Old Noshie and Skirty Marm turned pale. Could they be getting their stockings back at last? Mrs Tucker had kindly knitted them replacements (which they were wearing now), but these were not the same. Real witch-stockings are very tough, almost like boots.

Badsleeves grinned. "I'm not going to give you back your red stockings. I'm going to replace them – with these!"

From the ragged cushion, she picked up two new pairs of GREEN STOCKINGS.

This was a sensation. It had never happened before, in the whole history of Witch Island – an early Promotion, which would give two young Red-Stockings all the powers and privileges of Greens. The reporters in the Press Gallery were going crazy, and the crowd (apart from one or two sour old Purples) was cheering itself hoarse.

Old Noshie and Skirty Marm took off Mrs Tucker's red stockings, and dazedly pulled on the new green stockings.

"Is this a dream?" asked Old Noshie.

"We're GREENS!" cried Skirty Marm gleefully. "We can park our brooms in the palace railings and drop litter!"

It was a huge honour. After the ceremony, the witches and Mendax were hemmed in by admirers. Mendax was dragged away to a cat-party in one of the old slave tunnels. Witches of every stocking-colour queued to congratulate the new Greens. Over and over again, people told them they were saviours and heroes and wonderful and marvellous – until Old Noshie and Skirty Marm started to believe it. Tranters End seemed very far away. Mr Babbercorn and Mr Snelling did not call them wonderful or marvellous. What did they know? How could mere humans understand?

"Let's have some Nasty Medicine," said Skirty Marm.

"Just what a witch needs after a shock like that," agreed Old Noshie.

"After all, we're not little Red-Stockings any more," said Skirty Marm. "Us GREENS are old enough to handle anything!"

At the State Banquet which followed the ceremony, Old Noshie and Skirty Marm each drank a whole bottle of Nasty Medicine. So did their old pal, Chancellor Badsleeves. I am sorry to say that they were all revoltingly tipsy.

When the clocks struck midnight, Badsleeves burst into tears and cried, "You're the besh frenge a wisht heverad—!" and then collapsed into a bowl of spider trifle, snoring loudly.

"Deary me," hiccupped Old Noshie,

"perhaps we'd better go home."

"Pooh to that!" sang Skirty Marm. "The night is YOUNG!" She picked up two more bottles of Nasty Medicine. "Let's sneak away from this boring banquet, and visit some of our old haunts!"

The "Cough and Spit" was a Red-Stocking drinking cellar. When Old Noshie and Skirty Marm rolled in, all their old friends were waiting to cheer them. They sat down with Binbag, and her cave-mate Moonbott, and chatted about old times.

Suddenly, Skirty Marm gave Old Noshie a sharp nudge. "Look over there!"

She pointed to a large table in the corner. Around it, six witches were playing SQUITBLAT. This was a popular gambling game, played with cards and stone counters – and Skirty Marm had always fancied herself as a bit of a Squitblat expert. Mr Babbercorn, who hated gambling, would have been horrified to see the two witches joining the game. He would have been even more horrified to see them ordering several more bottles of Nasty Medicine.

Skirty Marm was good at Squitblat, so Old Noshie was not surprised to see her winning a pile of stone witch-money. The surprise was Old Noshie, who had never won a game of Squitblat in her life. Today, she could not stop winning. Very proud of herself, she scooped all the money into a small sack.

"I'm a RICH WITCH," Old Noshie said, with a giggle. "Well, I'm off now, Skirty. I'm getting some fresh air, some grub and another bottle of medicine. Coming?"

"No," said Skirty Marm, deep in her cards.

So Old Noshie went off exploring by herself. Normally, she would have been too timid to explore without Skirty Marm, but the Nasty Medicine had given her a false and foolish courage. If only she had been sober, she would have remembered how risky it was to visit the docks after dark. The Witch Island Docks were the roughest place on the Island – noisy, smelly, crowded and full of thieves and murderers.

With no very clear idea in her fuddled head of how she had got there, Old Noshie gaped around her. Gangs of sailor-witches, covered with tattoos, pushed past her in the narrow streets. The great wooden masts of the ships towered above a jumble of black rooftops. A fight was starting on the other side of the street. Old Noshie wanted to get away from the pushing and shouting. She stumbled through a door with a faded sign above it that said, *The Gastric Ulcer – Bar Snacks – Medicines*.

She was in a low sailors' tavern, very dark and full of smoke. The only customers appeared to be two very dirty, wrinkled old witches. One wore a black patch over one eye; the other had a hook instead of a hand. Both were smoking pipes. When these two witches saw Old Noshie, they stopped talking. The witch with the eyepatch hastily hid something in her lap.

Old Noshie was not a brave witch, and she did not like the look of these two characters. But there was a stout bottle of Nasty Medicine on the table between them, and she did like the look of that.

"Well, well!" chortled the Eyepatch witch, her one eye gleaming. "If it ain't Old Noshie, the National Heroine! Do two old sailors an honour and have a drink with us!"

Old Noshie wasn't sure, but thought one little drink could not do any harm. After four little drinks, she had decided that the two old sailors were her favourite witches in the world. She insisted on buying them another bottle of Nasty Medicine. The sailors licked their lips greedily when she produced the little sack full of her Squitblat winnings.

They began to ask Old Noshie all kinds of searching questions about herself. It was not long before Old Noshie began to talk about marrows. Eyepatch said it was a dreadful shame her marrow wouldn't grow.

"You know, Noshie," Eyepatch said, "you should use a spot of magic!"

Old Noshie shook her head. "I can't. Our curate has got ever so good at recognizing all the OBVIOUS sorts of magic."

"Then it's a very good thing you ran into me and my mate," Eyepatch said. "We've got a spell your curate-bloke will never notice – it's not obvious magic, by any means." She winked hard with her single eye. "We're in a bit of a hurry to get rid of it. Our ship sails tonight, and we don't want it to fall into the wrong hands."

Old Noshie was not a quick-witted witch, but she understood that Eyepatch wanted to sell her a black-market spell.

Eyepatch, cackling wickedly, pulled a small velvet bag from her rags. "Take a look at this, Noshie. It's the very latest in Growing-charms! A friend of ours stole – ahem! – BORROWED it from a research lab at the University."

Old Noshie stared fearfully at the bag. Buying or selling illegal spells was a very serious crime on Witch Island. And Mr Babbercorn was bound to disapprove. But she couldn't help thinking how splendid it would be to collect the silver cup for the prize marrow. If nobody would be able to tell she had used magic, where was the harm?

"This will make anything grow," whispered Eyepatch into Old Noshie's guilty green ear. "As much or as little as you want. Have a look!" She gave the velvet bag to Old Noshie.

On Witch Island, valuable spells and charms are often made of precious stones, and beautifully carved.

Old Noshie carefully took out the Growing-charm. It was about the size and shape of a hens' egg, completely covered in emeralds. Between the rows of jewels, in tiny writing, were the instructions for using the charm with a standard Biggening spell.

"Pretty, ain't it?" asked Eyepatch, taking it back. She nudged her friend, and the witch with the hook grunted. "Worth a small fortune, that is."

"I haven't got a fortune," said Old Noshie.

The sailor-witches laughed, in a way that was rather horrible. Old Noshie tried to join in, but her voice came out high and wobbly.

"What you've got in your purse will do," said Eyepatch.

She grabbed Old Noshie's sack of money and dropped the stolen charm into her lap.

The two sailor-witches stood up.

"Wait!" cried Old Noshie. "How do I know this thing's not DANGEROUS?"

"Ha ha! You DON'T!" screeched Eyepatch.

And both witches suddenly vanished into thin air.

3

A Cold Spell

Old Noshie woke up next morning feeling terrible. She was lying in a gutter near the palace, with no idea how she had got there.

"How could I have been so stupid?" she moaned to herself. "Why did I drink all that Nasty Medicine? Deary me – I'll never touch another drop again!"

All at once, the memory of last night came rushing back to her, and she shuddered. It was incredible – she could hardly believe it. Easygoing, timid Old Noshie had played Squitblat, skulked around the docks, and bought a black-market charm from two sailor-witches. If Mr Babbercorn ever found out, he would be scandalized.

Old Noshie was deeply ashamed of herself. She felt in her pocket for the stolen charm. Yes, it was still there. She knew she ought to take it straight to the police – and then into her mind popped a vision of her marrow.

She saw it, green and plump, wearing a red rosette that said "1st Prize". She saw it surrounded by admiring humans. She couldn't wait to tell Skirty Marm – that silver cup was as good as won. Smiling to herself, Old Noshie tucked the charm into the secret pocket inside her vest and strolled into the palace to find her friends.

The palace was in a dreadful mess after last night's party – littered with bat-bones, empty medicine bottles and snoring witches. Mendax and Skirty Marm were in the old throne-room, sipping cups of warm rainwater.

"Morning!" beamed Old Noshie. "Blimey, Skirty – where are your clothes?"

Skirty Marm was wearing nothing but her new stockings, a pair of long bloomers and a vest.

"I lost everything at Squitblat," Skirty Marm said gloomily. "I would have lost these bloomers, too, if the police hadn't raided the cellar and stopped the game."

Mendax shuddered. His eyes were hidden by dark glasses. "This place is so SORDID! Thank

goodness Miss Binbag offered to fetch you some more rags – because I refuse to fly home with a half-naked witch!"

"I had a brill time last night," Old Noshie said. She nodded in a meaningful way at Skirty Marm to show she had a secret to tell.

"Stop pulling silly faces at me!" snapped Skirty Marm. "Mr Babbercorn was right, and I should have listened to him. Gambling is a STUPID way to lose your money. Nasty Medicine gives you nothing but a big headache. From now on, I'm going to be good all the time."

Old Noshie was alarmed. "ALL the time?"

"Yes," Skirty Marm said firmly. "No more wild witch parties. No more magic."

"No magic!" squeaked Old Noshie. This could be tricky. Skirty Marm being good meant no help with the charm – and Noshie was not at all sure she could make it work on her own.

"What's the matter?" asked Skirty Marm.

"Nothing!" said Old Noshie, feeling her pocket nervously. Her green face blushed the colour of a Savoy cabbage.

Skirty Marm did not notice how shifty Old Noshie looked, because Binbag arrived at that moment with the spare clothes. Skirty Marm put them on with a lot of grumbling about the quality of the material. The ragged dress was skimpy and showed too much bloomer, but the hat was in the latest fashion (wide brim, narrow point) and rather smart. Skirty Marm studied her reflection for a long time and tried the hat at several angles until Mendax spat, "Is this a fashion show? I want to go home!"

Skirty tore herself away from the mirror, and the two witches and Mendax made their way down to the palace beach. A large crowd had gathered to see them off, but there was no more cheering. Every witch on the Island was feeling fragile after the celebrations. This crowd was so quiet you could hear every rasping note of the Pock-horn band.

The Chancellor (with a bag of ice under her hat to soothe her sore head) solemnly smacked them all goodbye. Mendax fitted on his miniature crash helmet and climbed into his basket. The witches mounted their brooms.

"Goodbye!" called Chancellor Badsleeves. "Come back for Explosion Day next year!"

The Pock-horn band played, "Will ye no come back again?" The two brooms leapt up into the grey air and shot out over the sea.

Skirty Marm and Old Noshie perked up when the smells of an English summer wafted through the warm air. Witch Island had been fun, but they were longing for the peace and quiet of home.

Mendax took off his dark glasses. "Ah, my beloved! I shall lay all my honours at her little ginger feet! What do I care for prizes if they do not please fair Gingersnap?"

"I can't wait to see Mr B.—" began Old Noshie, then stopped suddenly. How could she face Mr Babbercorn when she was planning to do something wicked?

All the Babbercorns and Mr Snelling rushed out of the vicarage as soon as the two brooms landed on the lawn. Beaming with pride and happiness, the three heroes gabbled out the news about their amazing honours. The vicar was delighted to have a titled cat.

"When you get married, your wife will be LADY MENDAX!" he giggled. "How splendid!"

"Mr Snelling – spare my blushes!" Mendax murmured. "I haven't asked her yet!"

Mr Babbercorn and Alice were very impressed by the witches' new green stockings.

"This shows that the other witches respect you," said Mr Babbercorn. "They trust you not to do anything dodgy!"

He meant it as a joke, but his words were torture to guilty Old Noshie.

"I can't go through with it!" she thought miserably. "I'll tell Mr B. everything!"

But she thought she would slip out and take a look at her marrow first.

There it lay, green and gleaming, in its soft bed of soil. But when Old Noshie measured it, she was dismayed to find it had not grown a single millimetre. Very slowly, with a thumping heart, she pulled the stolen spell out of her vest. The emeralds winked in the warm afternoon sunshine.

Old Noshie could not resist. She adjusted her eyes to read the tiny writing (witches can improve their eyesight by pulling their ears) and did her best to take in the instructions. It was easier than she had expected. The magic part of the charm was stored in the form of a mist inside the egg-shaped case. It could be released by a

gentle squeeze of the hand, while reciting the standard Biggening Spell.

Old Noshie's only problem was remembering the standard spell.

"Drat – I wish I could talk to Skirty Marm," she thought. "She'd know how to do it!"

"Noshie!" Alice's voice called, across the garden. "Tea's ready!"

"Coming!" gasped Old Noshie. In a panic, she gabbled what she hoped was the spell and squeezed the charm above the marrow. The charm turned warm against her hand, then icy cold. A wisp of green smoke swirled over the flower bed for a moment, and vanished.

"Right," said Old Noshie, frowning at the marrow. "Start growing!"

Biting, freezing cold woke the witches in the belfry next morning. Their noses were frozen, the bells were hung with icicles. The world outside lay under a thick white blanket of snow.

"Brrrr!" said Skirty Marm. "What's going on?"

Her teeth chattering, she went over to one of the big windows.

"You don't get snow in JUNE!" said Skirty Marm.

Old Noshie jumped out of bed. "Skirty – the marrow! Mr Fisher said they don't like the cold!"

The witches leapt on their broomsticks and swooped down to the snowy vicarage garden. To their huge relief, their marrow looked as healthy and glossy as ever. Skirty Marm went into the house to borrow one of Thomas's baby-blankets to wrap around the marrow. While she was gone, Old Noshie measured the big green vegetable. She was terribly disappointed to find that it had not grown.

"Perhaps," she whispered hopefully to herself, "it takes a couple of days to work."

At least her precious marrow had not suffered in the freakish weather. The cold weather had attacked strawberries, roses and geraniums like knives. Nobody could explain it, and when the villagers found that the snow was only over Tranters End (it stopped at the boundaries of St Tranter's parish), they could not help suspecting the witches. How else could you explain snow in June?

Mr Babbercorn spent the whole day assuring

people that Old Noshie and Skirty Marm were completely innocent. "They'd never do anything to harm their marrow," he pointed out. "And they don't get up to that sort of mischief any more."

Privately, he begged the witches to confess if they had been mucking about with the weather.

"Mucking about?" cried Skirty Marm. "Us? Never!"

"Never!" echoed Old Noshie.

"We haven't performed a single spell since we came home," Skirty went on. "Have we, Nosh?"

"Oh, I believe you," Mr Babbercorn said happily. "And I'm so proud of you for giving up your witchy ways!"

Neither he nor Skirty Marm noticed that Old Noshie's green face had gone as pale as a peppermint cream.

4

Deep Trouble

The freakish weather continued through the next day. The people of Tranters End turned on their central heating and took out their thick winter jumpers. Although Mr Babbercorn did his best to proclaim the innocence of the witches, a cloud of suspicion still hung over them. This made Skirty Marm very indignant, and Old Noshie very shifty. She had begun to wonder if the frost could have anything to do with her black-market spell.

On the evening of the second day, as the sky darkened, a new light was noticed high in the night sky. This time, it was not only above Tranters End – there was something about the strange new star on the television news.

Next morning, Mr Snelling woke before dawn with a feeling that something was NOT RIGHT. First, he realized that his nose was no longer frozen, which meant that the snow had gone and the temperature was back to normal. Second – far more shocking – Mendax's basket was empty. His tartan cat-duvet and tiny hot-water bottle lay just where the doting vicar had placed them the night before. He had not come home!

In a sudden panic, Mr Snelling pulled on his dressing gown and rushed outside into the grey half-light.

"Mendax!" he called. "Are you there? OW!" The ground fell away under the vicar's slippers. He rolled over and over until he found himself lying at the bottom of an enormous hole which had appeared in the vicarage lawn. The hole looked as if something as big as a house had burst out of it.

Mr Snelling's shouts of "Help! Help!" woke the Babbercorns and the witches. They all ran out into the garden and gaped in astonishment at the gigantic, yawning crater. How had this happened?

Old Noshie checked her marrow and was relieved to find it as healthy as ever, right on the edge of the hole. Mr Snelling looked very small down at the bottom of the deep pit, and he could not get out until Mr Babbercorn had fetched a long ladder.

"I'd better report this to PC Bloater," Mr Babbercorn said, in a worried voice. "It's certainly very odd. Witches—" He was very solemn. "You can tell me the truth, and I won't be angry. Have you been doing magic behind my back?"

"No!" cried Skirty Marm.

"No," mumbled Old Noshie, with her fingers and toes crossed. Now she was sure that all this upheaval must have been caused by her stolen spell, and she was suffering agonies of guilt.

"There must have been a tremendous explosion," said Mr Snelling, brushing soil from his dressing gown. "I wonder why none of us heard it?" A dreadful thought struck him. "Oh, witches – do you think Mendax could have been blown up?"

Skirty Marm did not like to see the kind vicar so worried. "Rubbish," she said stoutly. "That cat hasn't just got nine lives – he's got at least NINETY! Leave it to us – we'll soon find him! Won't we, Noshie?"

"Mmm-nnn-m," mumbled Old Noshie.

The moment it was properly light, the two

witches went down to the post office. It was not open yet, but Boots – the fat brother of Gingersnap, Mendax's girlfriend – was lying in a patch of sun on the windowsill.

"Good morning, Boots," Old Noshie said (witches can speak the language of any animal). "Have you seen Mendax?"

Boots slowly opened one cross green eye. "No," he said, in his deep, snarling mew. "And I don't want to see him. He shouldn't have come here – making eyes at my sister and turning her head with his fancy ways! Too good for us now, she is!"

"Go on, Boots," Skirty Marm said. "Be a sport. There's a kipper in it for you!"

Boots thought for a moment. Then he said, "All right. A WHOLE kipper, mind! Your pal Mendax had a quarrel with Gingersnap last night and rushed off saying all was at an end. Dunno where."

"I can guess," Skirty Marm said, relieved. "He'll be hiding in his Sulking Tree."

Mendax's Sulking Tree was a tall old oak, in the woods behind the church. Mr Snelling was not supposed to know that Mendax hid at the very top of this tree whenever he wanted to be alone.

"I'm very glad you told me," Mr Snelling said to the witches, at the bottom of the tree. "If he's broken up with Gingersnap, he needs me." He sighed. "Such a pity – I was looking forward to him having a wife and kittens!"

The roly-poly vicar was not fond of flying, but there was no other way to get him to the top of the Sulking Tree. Old Noshie and Skirty Marm stuck their brooms under his arms and flew him up to the highest branch.

At first, Mendax shouted, "Go away! Leave me alone to die of my broken heart!"

But as the vicar came nearer, he started to fuss. "Careful – he'll fall! Hold tight, Mr Snelling!"

The witches hauled Mr Snelling up on to the branch beside Mendax, and the heartbroken cat could not help jumping into the vicar's arms.

"It's all over!" he cried. "I asked Gingersnap to marry me – and she REFUSED!"

"Maybe she's found another cat," suggested Skirty Marm.

"She has NOT!" Mendax spat crossly, his whiskers bristling. "She says she can't marry me because I'm too far above her – I can talk

like a human, and she can only mew. She won't believe me when I say I love her just as she is!" He groaned. "I must learn to live without her. I may travel or take up some missionary work. If I can't live for Gingersnap, I must live for others!"

Mr Snelling blew his nose. He was deeply touched by his cat's goodness and bravery. "Witches, could you carry us down, please? This branch doesn't feel very safe."

Mr Snelling led the way back to the vicarage, holding his lovesick cat in his arms. "Hello!" he called, stepping through the back door into the kitchen. "I've found him!"

The kitchen was empty, and the house was strangely quiet.

"Hello!" he called again. "Cuthbert? Alice?"

After more silence, Alice's voice came from the sitting room. "We're in here!" She sounded odd – not exactly scared, but nervous.

Mr Snelling went into the sitting room and gasped, "Great Scott!"

At first glance, it looked as if someone had dumped a pile of rubbish in the middle of the sofa. At second glance, this turned out to be a witch – extremely ragged, and very, very old. Her ancient cloak and pointed hat were covered in cobwebs, and moths were fluttering around a battered carpet-bag at her feet.

"Professor Mouldypage!" cried the witches. She was the last person they had expected to see.

This ancient witch was the State Librarian of Witch Island, and a great scholar. Her knowledge of magic was immense. She was the only living witch who knew more about the Power Hat than Mrs Abercrombie had – and also the only witch who had been able to strike fear into Mrs Abercrombie's black heart.

The professor had visited Tranters End before.

"What a nice surprise," said the vicar politely, once he had recovered from the shock of finding the peculiar old witch on his sofa.

"She won't say a word to us," said Mr Babbercorn. "She's been waiting for Old Noshie and Skirty Marm."

Little Thomas was sitting on his lap. Thomas had grown into a toddler now, but he still used the language called "Babyspeak", which the witches could understand.

"Be careful," Thomas warned, in Babyspeak. "You two are in DEEP TROUBLE!"

Skirty Marm laughed. "Who, US? We're National Heroines! Dames of the Dustbin don't get into trouble!"

Professor Mouldypage raised her hand and pointed her gnarled old finger at Skirty Marm. "Insolent young witch," she croaked, in her rusty, creaking old voice. "The human child is right – you're in the deepest trouble of your lives! You could be stripped of your new green stockings for this!"

"Eh?" Skirty Marm was alarmed now. "What are you talking about?"

"You can hide nothing from me and my magical charts," said Mouldypage. "I know that someone here has used powerful magic to do a HORRIBLE thing. I have seen the signs of MRS ABERCROMBIE in the night sky!" She sniffed crossly. "In short, some dratted fool has managed to bring her back to life!"

This was a bombshell. Both witches turned deathly pale. Could this appalling news be true?

"Don't try to deny it," croaked Mouldypage. "I've been getting the signs on my radar since the day before yesterday. Someone has REBUILT Mrs Abercrombie, and the magic came from HERE!"

"Well, you're WRONG," Skirty Marm shouted furiously. "We haven't touched any magic – have we, Nosh?"

Old Noshie was trembling. "N-n-n—" she stammered.

"Come on, Professor!" protested Mr Babbercorn, trying to sound brave. "Mrs Abercrombie exploded into a million pieces! We all saw it. These two witches aren't nearly clever enough to put all that together!"

"Not on their own," said Mouldypage. She had very sharp black eyes among her wrinkles, and she pinned these on Old Noshie. "While you were visiting the Island, a valuable spell was stolen from a research-cave at the University. It was a spell designed not just to grow things, but to RE-GROW them too – from even the tiniest fragment."

"Noshie, what's the matter?" cried Alice, alarmed at Old Noshie's paleness and trembling. "Are you ill?"

The guilty green witch could stand it no longer. "All right!" she shouted, bursting into tears. "I did it! But they told me it was just a growing-spell people couldn't see! And I only put a little drop on my marrow!"

"You did WHAT?" shrieked Skirty Marm. "You old fool – there must have been bits of Mrs A. all over the garden! You've grown her instead!"

"I suppose that explains the funny weather," said Mr Snelling. "And the huge hole in the garden. It must be general upheaval due to vast and enormous magic."

"And it explains the new light in the sky," said Professor Mouldypage. "All my charts and instruments tell me that's none other than Mrs Abercrombie herself – alive and well and combing the Galaxy for the Glowing Stone! If she catches it, and turns it back into her Power Hat, we're all DOOMED!"

Witches, humans and cat went very quiet as they digested this terrible piece of news.

"It's all my fault!" sobbed Old Noshie. "I wanted to win the Marrow Cup, and instead I've brought Mrs A. back to life. Oh, Skirt – you'd better kill me!"

"Don't be silly," Skirty Marm said crossly. "Stop snivelling."

Mr Snelling stroked Mendax's warm black fur. "There must be something we can do."

"Absolutely nothing," rasped Mouldypage calmly. "Unless you go into outer space and catch that Glowing Stone before she does."

Skirty Marm stood up very straight and held her head high. "Then that's what we'll do!" she said proudly. "Noshie's a stupid old basket – but we're still a TEAM."

Old Noshie wiped her nose on her hat. "Thanks, Skirty."

Mendax leapt out of the vicar's arms. "I'd like to volunteer for the suicide mission too. What does it matter if I never come back?"

To everyone's surprise, the deep wrinkles of

Mouldypage's face squidged into what looked like a smile. "I thought you'd both stick with the idiotic green one, so I decided to give you one last chance. I haven't reported you to the Witch Police – I haven't even told anyone on the Island what I've seen in the skies. If you three can defeat Mrs Abercrombie one more time, nobody will ever know."

It was a very small chance, and it would involve the witches and Mendax in terrible danger, but Skirty Marm grabbed at it gratefully. "We're not disgraced yet! We still have our new green stockings! Now we can prove we're WORTHY of them!"

In the vicar's study (with the blinds drawn in case of enemy spies), Old Noshie and Skirty Marm adapted their broomsticks for space-travel, giving them extra super-strength so they would not break up when they went through the atmosphere. Mouldypage mixed an evil-tasting potion, which would have the same strengthening effect on the witches and Mendax.

Mouldypage then muttered a spell that gave Old Noshie and Skirty Marm flaps of extra skin on their necks, like the gills of a fish. With these, they would be able to breathe in space. For Mendax, she made a special backpack of oxygen and a space helmet that had once been the vicar's goldfish bowl.

By nightfall, everything was ready for the voyage. Alice, Mr Babbercorn and Mr Snelling were very afraid they would never see their magic friends again – the strange new light in the sky looked very sinister – but they did their best to be very cheerful and brave. They followed the witches and Mendax out into the dark garden and stood well back as the rocket-brooms took off in a great burst of flame.

"Good luck!" they cried. "Come back soon!"

Skirty Marm had been worried that she would cry, but she was too busy clinging to her broomstick. It shot upwards through the air like an arrow, gathering speed until she could hardly breathe. She felt a huge jolt and shudder as they went through the Earth's atmosphere – and then, suddenly, the roar in her ears turned to the deepest silence she had ever heard. Her broom had slowed down. Old Noshie's broom bobbed along beside her. They all stared, with open mouths, at the wonderful sights around them.

Planet Earth, and our moon, were far behind

them. They were drifting through a vast, humming blackness, where stars, planets and meteors sparkled like jewels. It was very cold. It did not feel as if they were travelling fast, but the stars fell away behind them with remarkable speed.

"Goodness, that was Pluto," said Mendax, his voice echoing in the vast emptiness. "We're heading out of our solar system – I hope someone remembers the way home!"

They were heading towards the sinister new light, where Mouldypage's runes and spells had said Mrs Abercrombie was to be found. This light, shining from a small new planet, was very bright – but there was something unsavoury about it, like the air around a bad fish.

For endless hours they flew through rocks and stars and clouds of glittering dust and never seemed to get any nearer. At last, they were close enough to plunge their broomsticks headlong into the planet's damp grey atmosphere.

"Hang on!" yelled Skirty Marm.

The two brooms shot through the atmosphere of this mysterious new planet and landed in a heap on something squashy.

5

Deep Space

The black ground was slightly sticky, slightly warm and very dirty.

"Yuck, what a stinky place!" said Skirty Marm. "No wonder Mrs Abercrombie chose it."

Old Noshie tried to sound casual, but her voice wobbled. "I – I wonder where she is?"

"We should be careful," Mendax said. "She might be watching us."

Skirty Marm stuck her broom into the soft ground. There was a loud rumble of thunder and the ground suddenly gave a great, shuddering heave, which flung the witches and Mendax right off their feet.

"Rather a BOUNCY place," remarked Mendax, steadying himself with his tail.

The strange, bouncy, wobbly ground stopped heaving. Skirty Marm dared to look around her at this peculiar new planet.

It was a bleak and lonely place, all black and grey, with damp air and very depressing scenery. As far as the eye could see, there were mountain ranges of grey and black. There was not one flower or green leaf, but there were trees of a sort – great forests of large, straight, grey trees, which seemed to be made of a rubbery kind of metal.

Old Noshie touched one of these trees and made a face – it had a very nasty stickiness.

"Look out!" yelled Skirty Marm. "Another earthquake!"

The ground was heaving again. The witches and Mendax were forced to cling to the nearest tree to stop themselves being shaken about like corks in a storm. Deep in the earth, far beneath their feet, there was a slow, rhythmic rumble.

"A tube train!" said Old Noshie knowingly – she had recently visited London.

"Don't be silly!" snapped Skirty Marm. "There's nothing like that here!"

Old Noshie scowled. "You don't know!"

"All right, smartie-stockings – where are the stations!"

The rumbling got louder. Mendax let out a "miaow" of fright. "Great heavens!" he gasped. "What a GHASTLY planet this is. No wonder Mrs A. ended up here!"

"Well, she can't have got the Glowing Stone yet," Skirty Marm said grimly, "or she'd have KILLED us ages ago."

"It's getting dark!" moaned Old Noshie. "I don't like it!"

Above them, the sky was whirling away from the orange glow of the distant sun. The strange landscape was plunged into sudden night, and the witches had to light the ends of their fingers to see anything (this does not hurt witches as it would a tender-skinned human).

"Noshie, stop that moaning," Mendax's cross voice mewed in the darkness. "I'd like to point out that this whole situation is your fault – you might at least try to be brave!"

"Shut up!" shouted Skirty Marm. "This is an emergency – we shouldn't be squabbling!"

Mendax sighed. "You're right. I shan't say one word about Old Noshie being a STUPID, SPROUT-COLOURED OLD NOODLE until we get home."

"Hey—" began Old Noshie furiously. But before she could insult the snooty little cat, the sky whirled once more, the ground heaved, and the whole planet was suddenly bathed in dazzling sunshine. The three magic friends saw each other's faces again, looking scared and extremely dirty – there was something very grubby and smeary about this place.

Skirty Marm glanced up at the horizon. Against the bright sky, she saw the outline of two jagged mountains. Terrible fear clawed into her soul – she did not know why, at first. Then it came to her all at once. The mountains were the exact same shape as Mrs Abercrombie's hideous nose and chin.

"This isn't a new planet at all!" she cried. "It's – it's – MRS ABERCROMBIE HERSELF!"

"What?" asked Old Noshie, deeply puzzled. "Where is she, then? What are you talking about?"

"Oh, don't be ridiculous!" mewed Mendax.

"If that's her nose and chin," Skirty Marm said, "we must be standing on her shoulder!"

The thought was disgusting. All three of them chorused, "YEUCH!"

"That stolen spell was so powerful," Skirty Marm went on, "that it's cloned Mrs A. from a tiny piece and grown her to half the size of our moon!"

"Dear me," Mendax said. "I shudder to think what all those underground noises are then."

"Of course!" Skirty Marm jumped excitedly on the squidgy ground. "That rumbling must be Mrs A. snoring – which means she's asleep, so we've got time to hide before she sees us!"

"Hide WHERE?" Old Noshie asked doubtfully.

"I'm sorry," Mendax mewed. "I refuse to go up her nose. Or in her ear."

Skirty Marm flung a skinny leg over her broomstick. "We'll fly into her hair – but remember, no sudden movements that might be itchy! One scratch, and we're all history!"

Mrs Abercrombie's hair lay beyond two mountain ranges. Old Noshie and Skirty Marm kept their brooms close to the ground. Knowing that the dreary landscape was Mrs Abercrombie made it look even uglier. It was not a pleasant flight. There were hills of flab, lakes of dribble, and warts the size of small castles.

To reach the thick grey forest of hair, they had to fly over Mrs Abercrombie's face. Old Noshie and Skirty Marm tried very hard not to look down, in case the repulsive sight made them faint and topple off their brooms. Mrs Abercrombie's nose was a steep crag that cast a huge shadow. They had to fly higher now to avoid the fierce gale blowing from her mouth and nose as she snored. They had to shut their eyes when the sun caught her metal teeth.

The witches landed at the top of Mrs Abercrombie's forehead and crept cautiously into her grey, tangled forest of hair. At every step they were terrified that the gigantic witch would wake and find them or (just as bad) suddenly scratch them off her head. Skirty Marm sat down against one of the trees, doing her best to forget that it was one of the old monster's hairs.

"If we manage to survive this," she announced, "I'm retiring – no more magical adventures. I've really had enough of magic now."

"Me too," agreed Old Noshie.

Mendax sighed. "I told Gingersnap I'd give up magic for ever if she'd marry me. I even told her I'd stop talking to humans."

"Ha! That'll be the day!" chuckled Old Noshie. "You couldn't stop talking if they made it illegal!"

Mendax coldly ignored this. "It was no use. Poor Gingersnap just couldn't believe that an innocent little country-cat like her could make me happy. I blame that brother of hers."

The last sentence was drowned by a long, deafening peal of thunder. Planet Abercrombie bucked and rolled until the witches and Mendax were bumped black and blue. Mrs Abercrombie had woken up. The sky was suddenly filled with a great, evil, familiar VOICE.

"I've grown again!" it roared. "When I get my Glowing Stone, I'll make them rue the day they threw ME off my throne! I shall crash into the miserable planet Earth, killing millions of stupid humans and making the rest into my SLAVES! Hahahaha! And every witch on Witch Island will bow down and worship me – not just as their QUEEN, but as their GOD! Hahahaha!"

The witches and Mendax stared at each other in despair. They had heard her plan. The whole Earth, and all the humans they knew and loved, were in mortal danger. And only two junior witches and one small cat stood between them and destruction. Though none of them dared to say it aloud, they all had the same thought: "We MUST try to save them – even if it KILLS us!"

"HahahahaHA!" laughed the shuddersome voice of Mrs Abercrombie.

"We can't do anything here," whispered Skirty Marm when the racket had died down. "Let's go!"

Mendax jumped into his basket. Old Noshie and Skirty Marm turned their rocket-brooms to full power. Flying away was a serious risk, especially now that Mrs A. was awake. Enormous as she was, she was bound to feel something when the flames shot out at take-off. Could they escape before she had time to notice them?

The brooms shot upwards into the grubby

grey sky of Planet Abercrombie. They were only just in time – as they zoomed through the atmosphere, an angry shout howled around them like a gale. The witches drove their brooms as fast as they could go and did not stop for a rest until they were several million miles away from Planet Abercrombie. Then they halted, on a globular cluster of stars near Jupiter.

Far away, through the mysterious universe, they saw a beautiful planet like a blue and green jewel.

"How pretty," said Old Noshie, "I should like to live there!"

"You DO live there, you goon," said Mendax. "It's EARTH." He let out a sob, which he turned into a cough. "Look at it, so calm and lovely! Imagine it smashed by that monster! What chance do we have to save it? We'll never find the Glowing Stone before she does!"

"Yes we will!" Skirty Marm said bravely.

Mendax shook his small, black head. "I must say, Skirty Marm, you impress me. Now that we are all about to die, I feel I should say how much I have always admired your plucky spirit. But even you have to admit, it's all impossible."

Skirty Marm was frowning her stubborn frown. She was not a witch who gave up easily. "That Glowing Stone used to be the Power Hat," she said thoughtfully. "And whatever it was, we never understood all its mysteries. But it has been very nice to us. I wish there was a way of asking it to help us now."

She sprang to her feet and startled Old Noshie by giving her a tremendous thump on the back. "Wait a minute – that's it!" she gabbled excitedly. "Don't you remember the way the Glowing Hat – I mean the Power Stone – hated Mrs Abercrombie? It burnt itself to ashes to stop itself going back to her! When it lived at Tranters End, it said it liked the humans and wanted to be GOOD!"

If cats had eyebrows, Mendax would have raised his. "So?"

"The Stone – or the Hat – works in ways that nobody understands," said Skirty Marm, breathless with excitement. "I'm going to try ASKING it to help us."

Mendax said sarcastically, "Do you have its phone number?"

"Quiet, cat," said Old Noshie, "unless you've got a better idea." She did not understand a word of the plan, but could not let Mendax take this lofty tone with her friend.

"That Stone can hear things," Skirty Marm said. "It can FEEL things and THINK things – even though everybody treats it like a box of tricks." She clenched her fists. "If I beg it to help the humans and the Earth, I really think it might listen!" She shut her eyes tight and concentrated harder than she had ever done in her life.

"This is ridiculous," snorted Mendax. "It'll never work."

"Shhhh," whispered Old Noshie. "Don't spoil it!"

The little cat shrugged rather scornfully. "Oh, well. What have we got to lose?"

"OW!" screamed Skirty Marm.

Something had stung the palm of her hand, very hard.

Old Noshie and Mendax stared as Skirty opened her hand to see what had hurt her. There, in her leathery palm, lay a jewel. It was a bit like a diamond, a bit like a pearl, and a bit like a drop of dew on a spider's web in the rising sun. It glowed with an eerie, silvery light. Mendax shaded his eyes with one paw, and Old Noshie's mouth hung open like a letterbox. This was incredible – Skirty's mad act of faith had worked. The wondrous Glowing Stone had heard her plea and travelled through space to find them.

Skirty Marm kissed it. "Oh, Stone! Thanks for coming!" She frowned rather anxiously. "Now, I wish I knew what to do with you!"

6

Battle in the Stars

Time on Earth and time in outer space move at very different rates. While the witches and Mendax were away, nearly a week had passed in Tranters End. Their human friends at the vicarage were dreadfully worried about them, but they had to pretend nothing was wrong – nobody else in the village had any idea that the wickedest witch in the world was on the rampage again.

Alice told anyone who asked that Old Noshie and Skirty Marm were visiting a friend on Witch Island.

Mr Snelling told people that Mendax was away at a Health Farm.

"I hate lying," he said miserably to Mr Babbercorn and Alice, "but nobody must guess what has happened. They've met Mrs Abercrombie, don't forget – they'd only be terrified, and what good would that do?"

Mr Babbercorn nodded sadly. "A panic is the last thing we need. We'll just have to carry on lying."

The tender-hearted vicar blew his nose. "I just wish," he said tearfully, "that I could say a few words of comfort to poor little Gingersnap. She's pining for my Mendax!"

Mr Snelling knew how Gingersnap felt. He missed Mendax too. On the sixth day of waiting and worrying, he went down to the Post Office and General Shop for some soap and a packet of cornflakes. This sort of shopping was usually done by Mendax, and Mr Snelling sighed as he thought of his beloved talking cat, pulling his small blue shopping-cart down the street.

Gingersnap was sitting on the post office windowsill. The romantic vicar thought he saw a look of lovelorn misery in her green eyes (female gingers are rare, and Gingersnap was very beautiful). Her silky, marmalade-coloured tail drooped sadly. Mr Snelling gave her a friendly stroke as he passed.

"Poor Ginger," said Mrs Tucker, "I know she's sorry she turned him down – I wonder if Mendax was right, and she let her brother bully her into it? She can't talk, but I could swear she understands every bit as much as Mendax!"

On his way out of the post office, the vicar halted beside Gingersnap. His round cheeks turned rather pink. He glanced up and down the street, to make sure nobody was watching, then he crouched down and muttered, "Look – er – Gingersnap – I've no idea how much you understand, or if what I'm saying sounds like gobbledegook – I mean, you're just an ordinary sort of cat (no offence). But let me assure you, Mendax still loves you! Please don't keep up this rubbish about you not being good enough. He loves you exactly as you are, and he wouldn't change you for the world!"

Was it his imagination, or did Gingersnap's ears twitch in a hopeful way? Mr Snelling felt a shade less miserable. He had set his heart on the two cats getting married and filling the vicarage with beautiful kittens. He wished more than ever that the three magic friends would come home safely, as soon as possible.

Apart from anything else, there was the problem of Mouldypage. The dusty old witch was staying in the spare bedroom at the vicarage. She was not easy to live with, treating

285

them all like servants and asking for disgusting things to eat (for instance, mashed slugs in a cobweb gravy). Mouldypage refused to be kept hidden away, but liked to walk around the village, scaring people by suddenly glaring in at their windows. Alice was always having to apologize for her peculiar old guest. She explained that Mouldypage had done a cave-swap with Old Noshie and Skirty Marm while they were visiting Witch Island.

Mouldypage was very nosy and asked endless questions about human life. Why didn't humans

eat hedgehogs? Why were they always asleep at night? On the afternoon of the village Flower Show, Mouldypage wanted to know what was so special about flowers when you didn't eat them?

The people of Tranters End were well used to Old Noshie and Skirty Marm, and were very fond of them. But they did not know what to make of this grumpy, crusty, eccentric old witch in her sagging, holey purple stockings. She made them nervous when she told them she was nine hundred and eighty-seven years old and remembered the French Revolution "like it was yesterday".

The yearly Flower Show, which included the Marrow Cup, was held in a large, striped tent in the big field behind the vicarage. Outside the tent there were stalls selling tea and cakes, and a brass band ("Where are the Pock-horns?" asked Mouldypage). The day was warm and sunny, and the whole scene looked very festive.

Alice sighed, thinking how much the witches had loved their marrow. "If only they were here! If only they could see how beautifully their marrow has grown!"

"Yes," Mr Babbercorn smiled, a little sadly.

"We took such good care of it and wheeled it here in Thomas's buggy – it was the least we could do for them." He glanced at his watch, saw that it was time for Prizegiving and signalled to the vicar. Mr Snelling hastily finished his scone and stepped onto a wooden platform at one end of the tent. There was a public address system he had borrowed from the vicar of the next-door parish. It was very old, and it startled Mr Snelling when it squealed, "OO-EE-OO-EE-OO-EE!"

"Ladies and gentlemen," said the vicar into the microphone, once the squealing had died down, "welcome to the Tranters End Flower Show. As usual, it is my job to announce the prizes awarded by our judges. We begin with the Mrs Lumsden Book Token for Lupin of the Year—"

He was interrupted by a loud voice, crackling through the speakers on the platform.

"Hurry up, SLOWCOACH! What's the matter with that broom of yours!"

"Skirt!" shouted little Thomas, clapping his hands in delight.

"They're back!" cried Mr Snelling.

Skirty's voice came again. "We should be

down in Tranters End at any min— Aaargh! –
WATCH OUT FOR THAT TENT!"

Above them, there was a tremendous ripping
sound. Through the striped roof of the tent –
smeared with dirt and smoking slightly –
crashed Old Noshie, Skirty Marm and Mendax.

When Mouldypage saw the Glowing Stone and
held it in her knobbly hand, all she would say
for ages was, "Well, well, well!"

Witches, humans and cat watched her
anxiously, waiting for the clever old witch to tell
them what to do next. They had all slipped away
from the Flower Show during the brass band's
concert and were having a private conference in
the vicar's study. Skirty Marm had told the
humans of Mrs Abercrombie's evil plan, and
they were all very pale and worried. Alice was
holding Thomas very tight and looked as if she
might cry.

"What can we do!" Skirty Marm asked
impatiently. "How can we stop Mrs
Abercrombie?"

"You must FIGHT her," Mouldypage
croaked solemnly.

"What?" squeaked Old Noshie. "Fight HER?

Just the three of us?"

Mouldypage was stern. "Just ONE of you, for it is written in the Great Parchment that the last battle must be single combat." She shot out her tongue and swallowed a passing bluebottle. "Normally, I'd say you didn't stand a chance. But you have the Glowing Stone and it seems to like you. It might decide to obey you, even if you can't put commands into the correct code."

She held up the stone. It filled the room with its soft, eerie, silver light. "Who is it to be?"

"ME," said Skirty Marm bravely.

"Oh, no!" wailed Old Noshie. "It should be ME because this is all my fault!"

"I too am filled with a sense of noble self-sacrifice," Mendax said heroically, "but I'll try not to let it lead me into doing something foolish. Skirty Marm is obviously the best witch for the job."

"Thanks, cat," said Skirty Marm. She shuddered. Even when armed with the Glowing Stone, facing Mrs Abercrombie alone was a terrifying prospect.

"Oh, Skirty, please—" begged Alice. "Be careful!"

"What shall I do if she EATS you?" sobbed

Old Noshie. "I can never manage without you!"

"Skirty, we're all very proud of you," said Mr Babbercorn. "Be as brave as you can. Remember that the Glowing Stone is so beautiful because it is so GOOD – and that goodness must always beat wickedness in the end!"

"Bleuch!" shouted Mouldypage. "Stop this revolting human SLUSH! Prepare to send out your challenge!"

She pressed the Glowing Stone into Skirty Marm's hand.

"But I haven't a clue what I'm supposed to do with it!" cried Skirty Marm.

"Tell it what you want – and get going!" shouted Mouldypage.

"All right," Skirty Marm said bravely. She turned to the others, trying to keep the wobble out of her voice. "This is goodbye, then."

"I'm coming with you!" cried Old Noshie. "I'm not going to be left out of your last adventure!"

Mendax was already fitting on his space helmet. "All for one, and one for all," he mewed. "Vicar, if I don't come back – be KIND to Gingersnap!"

"I will!" promised Mr Snelling.

Their broomsticks were propped up outside the back door. The witches mounted – Old Noshie still sobbing and moaning, Skirty Marm grimly silent. Mr Babbercorn helped Mendax into his basket on the back of Old Noshie's broom.

Skirty Marm clutched the Glowing Stone and concentrated with all her might. "Stone, I don't know the right way to ask you, but this is an emergency. Take me to where I can have my final battle with Mrs A.!"

All at once, the world seemed to turn upside down. The witches just had time to hear Alice screaming, and Mouldypage saying "Whoops!", before they found themselves zooming somewhere beyond the Milky Way.

Old Noshie did not like being in outer space. She was just thinking how lonely it all was, when she realized Mendax was miaowing frantically behind her.

She looked over her shoulder to see what was the matter and yelled, "Oh NO!"

With a shaking hand, she pushed the radio-switch on her broom. "Skirt! Something awful's happened! We've got Mr Babbercorn!"

It was all too true. Dangling from Mendax's

basket was the limp, pale form of the weedy young curate.

"Oh, STOCKING-STITCH!" Skirty Marm swore furiously, looking round. "He'll die up here! Glowing Stone – for goodness sake – do something!"

Hovering in mid-space, the witches and Mendax watched breathlessly. Mr Babbercorn moaned and coughed, then began to breathe normally. The Glowing Stone had made him his own private atmosphere. He opened his eyes, and they nearly popped out of his head when he found himself clinging to the back of a broomstick in the middle of uncharted space.

"Am I dreaming?" he murmured.

"Sorry about this," said Skirty Marm, riding her broom alongside him. "You got caught up by mistake. We'd better take you home."

"Certainly not," said Mr Babbercorn boldly. "Now that I'm here, I'm staying. I wouldn't miss this for the world."

The Glowing Stone suddenly became beautifully warm in the palm of Skirty Marm's hand. She looked down at it, and was surprised to see it shining with a soft, pinkish light.

"Mr B.," she said slowly, "I think the Stone

brought you here on purpose!"

"It always did like you," Old Noshie agreed (Mr Babbercorn had once worn the Glowing Stone when it had taken the form of a woolly bobble hat for a while).

"We don't know what it's planning," said Mr Babbercorn, "but we know it's on our side!"

They all felt braver now, and more cheerful. Skirty Marm saw a large lump of rock nearby with a nice flat surface, and signalled to Old Noshie to land. They dismounted, and disentangled Mr Babbercorn from Old Noshie's broom. Once he had got over the shock, Mr Babbercorn found outer space fascinating. He discovered that he could jump enormous distances across the flat rock, sending up a shower of sparkling dust every time he landed. He could leap hundreds of feet off the ground. Something in the special air he was breathing made him feel incredibly strong. He felt he could have picked up an office block and hurled it a hundred miles.

Then, suddenly, he knew why he was there.

"Witches," he said, very gravely, "I think the Glowing Stone wants ME to fight Mrs Abercrombie."

The witches and Mendax gasped, astounded.

"But you're a human!" protested Old Noshie. "You'll never be able to fight her!"

"I'm ready now," said Mr Babbercorn bravely. "Far readier than Skirty Marm – the Stone has prepared me."

Skirty scowled. She could never let the curate face Mrs Abercrombie alone. "Rubbish!" she snapped. "Mrs A. would make mincemeat of you!"

Mr Babbercorn's face was full of determination and dignity, although his clothes were covered with stardust and his glasses were hanging off by one ear. He put them back on his nose. "If you don't believe me, ask the Glowing Stone!"

They all stared at the Stone, lying in Skirty Marm's hand. As they watched, it slowly turned from silvery white to a deep, soft crimson – then there was a sudden flash of red light around the curate's head.

Skirty Marm gasped. "You're right – it is you it wants!"

She was offended that the Glowing Stone thought she wasn't tough enough to fight Mrs Abercrombie, but she was also secretly relieved that she didn't have to.

"Please give the Glowing Stone to me," Mr Babbercorn said. He took it, and held it up. "Thanks for choosing me," he said to it. "Please give me a weapon."

A few sparks fizzed in his hand. Then they grew into long rays of white light, almost too bright to look at. These dazzling spears twisted themselves into a sword in Mr Babbercorn's hand. He waved the sword and leapt gracefully upwards. It was an amazing sight – one that the witches and Mendax would never forget. Mr Babbercorn was hopping through the sky, using stars as stepping stones. And with each hop, he grew, until he was as gigantic as Mrs Abercrombie.

He landed on a meteorite, and his voice was huge enough to make the whole universe ring.

"Mrs Abercrombie, I challenge you to single combat, to the DEATH! Come and fight me, if you DARE!"

"Are you calling me a COWARD?" roared the dreadful voice of Mrs Abercrombie. "We'll see about that!" Her terrible voice was inside their heads. It was all around them, filling the whole universe – it was everywhere.

Something bright was rushing through the sky towards them. Mendax and the witches huddled together in terror when they saw it was the vast form of Mrs Abercrombie.

A ball of fire shot out of her mouth, and screamed straight at Mr Babbercorn. His friends trembled, but he made his sword into a cricket bat and whacked the fireball straight back at Mrs Abercrombie. It hit her on the bottom, and she howled with pain and rage. This time a fiery eagle, four times the size of Mr Babbercorn, leapt out of her mouth. It rushed at Mr Babbercorn to tear him apart with its great claws of fire. Old Noshie wailed and covered her eyes. Skirty Marm turned ghostly pale, and Mendax shook like a leaf.

But Mr Babbercorn stood firm. He held up his silver sword. The monstrous, flaming eagle swooped down on him and its scorching breath was close enough to singe the curate's eyebrows.

"I have a bird more powerful than that!" Mr Babbercorn called to her.

He sliced through the darkness and neatly cut off the eagle's head. It changed into a silver dove, shining with a light that was very bright and extremely beautiful. The witches and

Mendax each felt that they could gaze at that silver dove for ever.

The effect upon Mrs Abercrombie was very different. She was very angry, of course. But there was something else. Her face turned the colour of the skin on porridge, and her mean beady eyes widened in sheer disbelief.

"I don't believe it!" muttered Mendax. "She's SCARED!"

"How can she be scared of that beautiful bird?" wondered Old Noshie.

Skirty Marm's piercing red eyes had been watching intently. "She knows that Mr B. and the Stone are working together as a team – it's obeying his THOUGHTS as soon as he has them. Mrs A. always had to cast complicated spells before she could get it to do anything!"

Mr Babbercorn climbed on to the back of the outsized silver dove, brandishing his silver sword like a Knight of the Round Table.

"You can't beat us," he said, in a great voice like calm thunder. "The Glowing Stone – which you TRAPPED in your power by making it into the Power Hat – has no intention of being a hat AGAIN. It has chosen me to fight for it, because I am a clergyman and it's my job to help it to be GOOD."

"NO!" screamed Mrs Abercrombie, in rage and anguish. "It's not true! You're lying! That Stone respects me for my brains! It admires me for my wickedness! Ever since I made it into my Power Hat, it has WORSHIPPED me as its QUEEN! I'll destroy you all! And I'll start with your STINKY LITTLE FRIENDS!"

"Witches – Mendax – take cover!" called Mr Babbercorn. They dived behind a boulder, just in time to shelter from a storm of enormous rocks and shooting stars. Mrs Abercrombie screeched with annoyance when her missiles failed to kill them.

"You've RUINED my Stone!" she screamed, in a towering passion. "You took it to live with the humans, and you turned it soppy and useless!"

"SURRENDER!" Mr Babbercorn cried. "Your days of evil are over!"

"Never – OW! What's going on?" the enormous, planet-sized, horrible face of Mrs Abercrombie went grey with fright and disbelief. "How DARE you?"

Old Noshie, Skirty Marm and Mendax began to laugh – Mr Babbercorn's magical sword had

begun to shoot out long ribbons of light that
zipped through the sky and wound themselves
around Mrs Abercrombie like strands of sticky
jelly. Soon, she was wrapped up like a huge,
wriggling cocoon.

"I won't let you kill her," Mr Babbercorn said
to the Glowing Stone. "I want you to find a way
of trapping her until the very End of Time! I
want you to programme her so that if she ever
comes near our lovely Earth again, she will
disintegrate into a million pieces!"

Before their astonished eyes, the magical
sword hopped out of Mr Babbercorn's hand,

turned itself into the biggest tennis racket that has ever been seen and whacked the trapped Mrs Abercrombie thousands of miles across the universe before neatly turning itself into a sword again. They watched, with open mouths and gaping eyes, as Mrs Abercrombie's jelly-covered figure disappeared into the far distance.

The sword returned to Mr B.'s hand and was a Stone again – pale and flickering, as if it were exhausted.

The friends from Earth all stood in the vast, humming quiet of the skies.

Old Noshie was the first to speak. "Where did she go?"

Mr Babbercorn took off his glasses and cleaned them with his handkerchief. "The Stone tells me she is trapped, for Eternity, in one of the rings of Saturn – going round and round, like a bundle of clothes in a washing machine. She won't be bothering us again." He laughed suddenly. "Not even if Old Noshie buys another illegal spell!"

This time, thanks to the kindness of the Glowing Stone, time had been altered so that the Flower Show was still going on when Mr Babbercorn and the magic trio arrived back in Tranters End. Everyone in the village now knew what had happened, and they burst into loud cheers when the broomsticks crashed to the ground in the big field.

There were hugs and kisses, and explanations. The villagers rushed to their homes to bring food and drink for a big, impromptu party. Once they realized that the evil Mrs Abercrombie was defeated and the Earth was safe, all they could think of was celebration.

"Witches," said Mrs Tucker, "I'd just like to say, it was a great day for Tranters End when the two of you came to live in our belfry." (There were cries of "Hear hear!" from the other villagers.) "We've had a few shocks and upsets, but you've taught us all that witches and humans can be the best of friends."

"Three cheers for Old Noshie and Skirty Marm!" shouted someone. "Three cheers for the Belfry Witches!"

Old Noshie and Skirty Marm were overcome. All they could do was smile and blush and bow their heads. It was a wonderful moment.

Mr Snelling stepped forward. "And now, the final Prize. Because of their hard work, and everything they've done for us – and just because we love them so much – the judges have decided to award the Tranters End Marrow Cup to Old Noshie and Skirty Marm!"

He handed the grand silver cup to Old Noshie. She had dreamed of putting it in the belfry, and now she glowed like a green traffic light with the sheer joy of it.

"You've all been so kind to us," Skirty Marm said, in an unusually shaky voice. "Me and Nosh are proud to belong to this lovely village. But I do think we've forgotten one thing." She turned to Mr Babbercorn. "May I have the Glowing Stone?"

Mr Babbercorn gave it to her. She cradled the Stone very gently in the palm of her hand.

"This is who – or WHAT – we have to thank," she said. "When I first knew this Stone, it was the Power Hat, and I thought it was wicked. I now know it was in Mrs Abercrombie's power then, and that it really wants to be very good. Stone, I have one last command for you – tell us something that we can do for YOU!"

The Glowing Stone suddenly shot out a glorious rainbow of lights. Like a hissing gust of wind, a great, sighing voice filled the air around them.

I have waited thousands of years for this moment – the moment I could ASK to be set free! If you set me free, I can go back where I belong – to the Hills Before Time!

"Well, off you go, then," said Skirty Marm, patting it. "And thanks for everything."

The wind fell silent. The Glowing Stone was gone. Skirty Marm and Old Noshie heaved big sighs of relief.

"I didn't like to say anything in front of it," Skirty Marm said, "but I'm glad to see the back of that Stone – it's caused nothing but trouble! Now both it and Mrs A. are history, we can all get on with living happily ever after!"

And that is exactly what they did. Old Noshie and Skirty Marm led a busy life in Tranters End – dabbling in mild magic, but staying off the heavy stuff. They had both had enough of adventures and thought their village the best place in all the universe. Surprisingly, Mouldypage agreed with them. The strange old witch retired from the State Library and bought an old shed in the woods outside Tranters End. She did not come into the village much, but pottered about contentedly among her books.

Mendax proposed to Gingersnap again, and this time she accepted. To the delight of Mr Snelling, they got married and produced a litter of five beautiful kittens – two ginger boys, and three little black girls. They all began life by mewing in the normal way, but it soon became clear that they could understand and speak English.

"They can speak cattish to their mother, and personish to their father," Mr Snelling would explain proudly to flabbergasted strangers who had heard the kittens singing along to their nursery rhyme tape.

"I believe I'm the happiest and luckiest cat in the world!" Mendax declared one day, when he and Mouldypage were having tea with Noshie and Skirty in the belfry. Inevitably, they fell to talking about Witch Island (now a dull but peaceful place), and the bad old days of the queen.

"We're definitely the happiest and luckiest witches," said Old Noshie, gulping down a live bat.

"Yes, it was a great day for us when we got

infected with nasty human habits," said Skirty
Marm teasingly, winking at Old Noshie and
Mendax. "All that niceness, and kindness, and
kissing and hugging—"

"And being helpful," said Old Noshie.

"And telling the TRUTH," added Mendax.

Mouldypage puffed calmly at her pipe.
"Maybe it's not so bad," she muttered.

"Yes," said Skirty Marm, laughing, "those
soppy human customs are the best ones, after
all!"

K. H. McMULLAN

Welcome to the Dark Ages, where dastardly dragons rule the land, and the life of a weedy boy named Wiglaf is about to change forever . . .

There's only one place an ordinary boy can learn to be a hero – the Dragon Slayers' Academy.

Join Wiglaf on his quest to take on tyrants and battle the most fearsome of beasts!

VIVIAN FRENCH

SHARP SHEEP

Prepare to be scared. A flock of sheep has never been so frightening!

Josh collects horror comics and he loves to terrify his brother Paul and his stepsister Mandy with scary stories – the more gruesome, the better.

So when the three are sent to Wales to stay with Grampy Jenkins, Josh starts to spin a scary yarn about the strange Balwen Black Mountain sheep that live around Grampy's farmhouse, and about Rhys the Fleece – the legendary devilish shepherd that guards them. He also tells of the Magic Wish of Rhys the Fleece – granted to anyone brave enough and strong enough to stay out in the valley all night long . . . and survive.

But as Josh, Paul and Mandy are about to discover in the cold, dark hills, the truth is usually far more horrifying than fiction . . .

A selected list of titles available from Macmillan Children's Books

The prices shown below are correct at the time of going to press. However, Macmillan Publishers reserves the right to show new retail prices on covers which may differ from those previously advertised.

K. H. McMullan

Dragon Slayers' Academy	0 330 43451 9	£4.99

Vivian French

Sharp Sheep	1 405 04783 6	£9.99

Susan Price

Olly Spellmaker and the Hairy Horror	0 330 42119 0	£3.99
Olly Spellmaker and the Sulky Smudge	0 330 41582 4	£3.99
Olly Spellmaker: Elf Alert!	0 330 42123 9	£4.99

All Pan Macmillan titles can be ordered from our website, www.panmacmillan.com, or from your local bookshop and are also available by post from:

**Bookpost,
PO Box 29, Douglas, Isle of Man IM99 1BQ**

Credit cards accepted. For details:
Telephone: 01624 677237
Fax: 01624 670923
Email: bookshop@enterprise.net
www.bookpost.co.uk

Free postage and packing in the United Kingdom